back in the rancher's arms

a Trinity River novel

back in the rancher's arms

a Trinity River novel

ELSIE
DAVIS

Entangled Publishing, LLC
2614 South Timberline Road
Suite 105, PMB 159
Fort Collins, CO 80525
Visit our website at www.entangledpublishing.com.

Bliss is an imprint of Entangled Publishing, LLC.
For more information on our titles, visit http://www.entangledpublishing.com/category/bliss

Edited by Heidi Shoham
Cover design by Bree Archer
Cover art from iStock

Manufactured in the United States of America

First Edition April 2018

Bliss
An Entangled imprint

As my debut novel, this story will always hold a special place in my heart. It was made possible through the endless support and love from family and friends, and from the many special people I've met along the way who took the time to help me learn how to write. RWA conferences, workshops, critiques, webinars, online classes, and editorial feedback have all been key components in my journey to realizing my dream. Thank you, everyone!

To my husband, Don, my source of inspiration and my own personal hero, thanks for believing and letting me chase the dream.

To one of my closest friends, Tricia Tyler, thanks for the endless hours of phone calls, our fabulous writer's getaway, and your never-failing support and belief that this was "the book."

To my fabulous editor, Heidi Shoham, thanks for believing in me and for falling in love with my story. Working with you has been amazing.

Chapter One

Kayla stepped out of her SUV and barely missed a steamy pile of horse manure. Too bad she couldn't avoid the crap she would step into coming home. She couldn't *not* come to her cousin's wedding, even if it meant facing Dylan for the first time in years, and it was time to break the news of the partnership she'd been offered to her parents.

She popped open the rear door and picked up her bags, careful not to lean against the dusty frame. The wheels of the heavy suitcase kept catching on small pebbles as she dragged it down the driveway to the front porch, balancing the garment bag across her shoulder. She entered the old house, the screen door slamming behind her.

"Mom, I'm home," she called out loud enough to wake the neighbors, even if they were a good half mile away. It was the only way to be heard above the noise of the oversize fan that sounded more like a John Deere tractor barreling through the living room.

Nothing in the room had changed since her last visit home at Christmas, but then, it never changed. Old furniture with faded fabric. Throw rugs covered scuffed and cracked wood floors. The baby cradle and wooden rocker handcrafted by her great-grandfather.

Three generations of Anderson family portraits lined up in a row, hung on the wall. Their calm faces judging. Always judging. Just like her parents.

And then there was her picture. The one who dared to leave.

"Mom. Dad. Anyone here?" she called again, this time from the base of the stairs leading up to the second floor.

"Kayla?" Her mother came through the kitchen door with a large bouquet of fresh-cut daylilies in one hand, the other arm wide and waiting.

Kayla inwardly chuckled when she saw her mother's outfit. White stars the size of Texas duplicated themselves all over the bright-red pantsuit; the homemade eyesore one of Kayla's least favorites.

"I can't believe you're here. And for a whole week. It's been a long time since you've been home." Her mother pulled her into a tight hug, but not before Kayla saw the mist in her eyes.

"It's good to see you, too. You know how it is, school and work keep me crazy busy. And being the new assistant at the vet clinic means low man on the totem pole when it comes to time off." Not to mention Riverbend, Texas, wasn't on her list of favorite places.

"I'm looking forward to when you graduate and move back home. The distance issue will be a thing of the past when you open a clinic in town. I thought when you got into vet school I'd see you more often since it's only a few hours away, but I understand."

Her understanding wouldn't last to the end of the weeklong visit. "Hmmm. Thanks."

"Let me put these daylilies in water and get the Elephant

Ears out of the oven. I made them just for you." Her mother paused at the door and glanced down the hall before entering the kitchen.

Puzzled, Kayla followed. "Yummm. I can't wait."

"I wasn't expecting you this early."

The familiar smell of vanilla and maple filled the room. Her stomach rumbled in anticipation of her favorite pastry. It was a popular treat, especially at state fairs, but no one could make them as good as her mother.

"I told you I'd be home around one. I'm only thirty minutes early."

"Perfect timing for a fresh, hot batch right out of the oven." Her mother moved the baked flat dough from the oven to the baker's rack. "Big and puffy, just the way you like them."

"Great. They smell amazing. Where's Dad?" Kayla asked, happy to have sidestepped the moving home comment.

"With the drought, nothing much makes him happy anymore. But finding out you were coming home for a week, well, that's made him happier than I've seen him in a good long time. He's probably still in the barn. I'll send..." Her mother's gaze darted over Kayla's shoulder, toward the kitchen door. A flicker of guilt flashed across her face.

"Send who?" Kayla asked.

"Ummm, nothing. I forgot something is all."

She picked up a warm pastry and blew on it. One bite, and her mouth exploded with the delicious taste of maple. Warm, sweet, and wonderful.

"Hmmm. These are as delicious as I remembered."

"I've got your favorite toppings. Chocolate and bananas."

"Then I'd have to wait until they cool." She laughed. "Maybe on the second one."

She often wondered about the secret ingredient her mother used, but every time she asked, the answer was always the same. Love.

"I'm glad you like them. There's something I need to tell you since you're here." Tight lines formed across her mother's forehead.

"Is everything okay?" Her mother sounded nervous, and it was unsettling.

"The thing is I didn't know he, I mean he—" Her mother's gaze shifted to the right, past Kayla.

"She's trying to tell you I'm here."

A wave of heat coursed through her veins. Her stomach pitched like it was falling from the top of the Grand Canyon into the deepest part of the ravine.

Dylan. Damn it. Dylan.

She swung around to face her first love. The man she'd given her virginity to. The man she'd been all too willing to give up her dreams to be with forever. The man who'd ripped her heart to pieces when he walked away and then betrayed her in the worst way possible.

He was the man who'd managed to get both her and her ex-best friend, Becky, pregnant.

"What are you doing here?" Contempt dripped from her voice, but the words fell flat. Five years to prepare a scathing remark and none of them surfaced to rip his heart out, to give him a small taste of the pain she'd felt when he walked away.

The urge to hurt overrode years of determined effort to forget him and move on. One small setback. She took a deep breath and tried to refocus her energy, to return to the hard-won inner peace she'd carved out for herself.

"Hello to you, too, Kayla." His familiar grin mocked her. "But to answer your question, I'm fixing the roof."

Tall, dark, and better than an Elephant Ear. Nothing puffy about him. Bulging pecs filled his T-shirt and made it look like it came from the boys' department. Rock-hard triceps stretched the cotton short sleeves to the limit. Jeans that dipped low in the front, weighed down by a large silver buckle with the letter *H* emblazoned across it.

Hunter. A few other *H* words came to mind. Handsome. Hunk. Hot. The list went on. History. Hurt. Hell.

And heartache. Don't forget the heartache.

It wasn't fair. She wanted him to be out of shape or balding, anything other than I-still-want-you sexy.

"Does it have to be done now? Maybe you can come back in a week?" Anything, as long as he didn't stay here. It was bad enough she'd have to deal with him at her cousin's wedding, anything else was beyond the realm of acceptable torture.

She was over Dylan, but it didn't mean she was ready to play nice. And it didn't mean her body had gotten the over-him message.

"I asked him to fix the roof, honey," her mother chimed in.

She shot her mother a pleading look. After all these years, surely her mother wasn't still holding out hope for her and Dylan to make peace with one another. But then again, she'd always liked Dylan, even when he'd broken Kayla's heart and walked away, her mother had defended him. But then again, her mother didn't have all the facts. No one did.

Resentment burned like bile. This wasn't the time or place to unload on the man she'd once thought of as her knight in shining armor but who had turned out to be nothing more than a self-serving rat. But it didn't have to stop her from taking back some of the dignity he'd stolen.

She plastered a smile across her face and looked squarely at her mother, fighting the urge to look at Dylan. A quick escape upstairs was her best bet to avoid the current situation. She picked up the garment bag, slung it over her shoulder, and reached for the large suitcase. "Right. I'll just take these up to my room." She was hoping Dylan would take the hint and leave.

"See you soon, Kayla," Dylan said before turning back to her mother. "Mary, the roof's mostly done, and I'll finish it up tomorrow morning. Thanks for the Elephant Ears. Derek and I always appreciate them."

Kayla paused at the doorway.

Since when had her mother started cooking for the Hunter brothers? And how dare Dylan ignore her request to stay away? He knew why she didn't want him here. At least half the reason anyway. *What is he up to?*

"If the roof is mostly fixed, there's no urgency. The forecast isn't calling for rain, so I'm sure you can leave it until after the wedding. It's going to be hectic around here, and having a repairman underfoot will only add to the stress." Kayla looked Dylan straight in the eye, challenging him to contradict her.

"Kayla," her mother choked out.

"It's okay, Mary," Dylan said. His intense gaze fixed on Kayla. "I'm not a repairman. I'm a friend of the family, and I'm fixing the roof to help my neighbors. And even though it hasn't rained in a long time, a storm can pop up without warning. You won't be able to get rid of me easily until after Saturday. No matter how much you want me gone," he added, his voice flat and final.

Kayla glanced uneasily at the stairs, eying her escape before she turned back to Dylan. Her curiosity slid into overdrive.

"Why not?"

If Dylan was going to be blatant, then so was she. She wasn't a naive schoolgirl anymore—her days of agreeing with him simply to earn his approval were over long ago.

"Haven't you heard?" The first hint of a smile tugged at his lips. Whatever he was going to say wouldn't be good. Kayla kept quiet, waiting for the proverbial cowboy boot to drop.

"I'm the best man at the wedding. I guess it's lucky for you I live next door, or I'd be sleeping in the guest room next to you."

Kayla closed her eyes and drew in a deep and ragged breath, trying to stop the rollercoaster of emotion rushing through her veins. Her heart galloped wildly out of control. No way. This couldn't be happening.

Best Man. Maid of Honor.

What the hell were her cousin and Ethan thinking?

Ethan, Casey, Dylan, Randy, and Tommy, otherwise known as the Fearless Five, always stuck together, but Ethan and his cousin, Casey, were like brothers. She'd mistakenly assumed he'd be the best man when she'd agreed to be maid of honor.

"Why is Ethan settling for second best? Is Casey unavailable?" She saw no reason to hide her disdain.

A pained look crossed Dylan's face. "Casey died in Afghanistan over a year ago. Guess you're stuck with me."

A sick feeling landed with a thud in the middle of her chest.

"What?" she gasped. "Casey?" She rubbed her arms, seeking warmth and comfort, anything to shield her from the truth of Dylan's callously delivered news. She looked to her mom for confirmation.

"I'm sorry, honey. It's true."

Fun loving, happy-go-lucky Casey is gone.

Dead.

She didn't come around much, but someone should have told her.

She'd followed the Fearless Five around for years, mostly because of Dylan, but the others had tolerated her presence, and she'd grown fond of them all. It had been like having five big brothers, at least until her feelings for Dylan had changed.

Remorse stuck in her throat, making it almost impossible to speak. The depth of pain in Dylan's voice had been real. Her heart ached for all the guys. Dylan included.

"I'm sorry. I didn't know." She reached out to touch his arm. She didn't have the heart to be mean after hearing the news. The guys must have been devastated, along with the entire town. Casey had been a down-home country boy, a lot like apple pie. He was sweet and could entice anyone who dared to resist his appeal.

It couldn't be any clearer she was no longer a part of the town. She was an outsider and couldn't remember feeling as alone as she did right now.

Strike that. There were two other times in her life she felt this alone, both Dylan's fault. Experience didn't make the pain any less to bear.

Dylan glanced down at her hand on his arm before leveling her with a hard glare.

"There's a lot you don't know. Maybe finally coming home you'll learn some of it." Dylan tipped his hat low, turned, and left.

There's a lot you don't know, either, you two-timing jerk.

Chapter Two

Kayla pushed open the door to her bedroom. For one second, it was like stepping into her childhood. Her favorite stuffed animals cluttered the bed. Posters of sexy cowboys lined the walls. A homemade blue denim bedspread covered the double bed, complete with matching curtains. Picture boards were only half covered with childhood photos, the other half were where pictures of Becky had long since been removed.

An empty hook stood out within the darkened space on the wall where a collage of Dylan photos once hung. Photos safely stashed in the back corner of her closet. Hidden from her view and hidden from her heart.

She hadn't planned on seeing a lot of Dylan, except at the wedding, but then she hadn't planned on Sophia getting married at her parents' farm, or him being the best man.

Kayla only ever stayed a matter of days when she visited, because every day longer in town meant a greater chance of running into Dylan or Becky. That was always enough to spur her into action, leaving the farm in a trail of dust reflected in the taillights of her hybrid SUV. No rusty beat-up Ford for her, please and thank you.

But this time she was determined not to let the past spoil her fun or rule her emotions. Dylan being best man would make it harder, but not impossible. She removed the emerald-green dress from the garment bag and carried it to the walk-in closet. She ran her fingers down the silky fabric and held it up against her body to see the reflection in the mirror. It was a gorgeous dress with the front hemline a foot higher than in the back, designed to show off her designer cowgirl boots.

A little class mixed with a little sass.

An image of Dylan dressed in a black tux, his hand on her waist as he led her around the dance floor, popped into her head. In perfect time, the two of them floated across the floor like Prince Charming and Cinderella at the ball. Except in her case, midnight arrived before the ball even started, and Dylan had chosen to dance with someone else.

Seeing Dylan again was playing havoc with her imagination, and it needed to stop. She would partner with Dylan at the wedding for Sophia's sake, but it didn't mean she had to like it.

* * *

Dylan pulled himself up into the saddle and headed for the ranch, giving Thunder his head.

Nothing about seeing Kayla again had gone as planned. He'd given up any claim on her when he walked away, but it hadn't changed his reaction when he'd come face-to-face with her. Desire had surged through his veins, as if the time apart hadn't existed.

Years ago, she'd forced him to see her as a woman, and since then, he hadn't been able to get her out of his mind. He'd always hoped one day she'd come home to stay, back to her roots. But his dream of her return didn't exactly mesh with reality. She'd shown him all too clearly she had no intentions of revisiting the past.

It had been easier to leave the house and give her space, than for them to have a confrontation while her animosity was in overdrive, not to mention with her mother looking on. If he had any chance of renewing their friendship, they would have to talk sometime, but today wasn't the day. And from there, anything else would have to be her decision. Her choice.

Dylan slid off Thunder and tied the horse's reins to the hitching post. He ran his hand down the horse's neck and patted his back. "Good boy. I'll be back in a minute to take care of you." The horse flicked his head as if he understood.

Dylan and Thunder worked together as a team day after day, doing hundreds of jobs on a never-ending list. But right now, the duty that needed his attention the most was one where his steadfast gelding couldn't help. It was a duty that took up more and more of his time lately and not in a good way.

He leaned in through the barn door and hollered. "Derek!" Dylan didn't see or hear his brother and took a few steps inside for a better look. School had been out for almost an hour, and the kid should have already been doing his chores.

The pitchfork lying on the ground meant he'd been here and left. There weren't enough fingers on two hands to count how many times he'd told his brother it was dangerous to leave the damn pitchfork lying on the ground with the prongs facing up. Thirteen years old and he ought to be able to figure it out by now.

"Derek!" he called, anger and frustration rolled into the name. Nothing.

He checked the tack room. It wouldn't be the first time he found him asleep in there.

Most parents would be concerned when their kid disappeared, but Derek made a regular habit of disappearing when there were chores to be done, usually only bothering to show up at suppertime.

Dylan headed for the house. "Derek!" he yelled out loud enough to be heard through the entire house, but he still proceeded to check every room. There was no guarantee Derek would answer. Stubborn boy. A trait they'd both inherited from their father.

Nothing.

Shaking his head, Dylan headed back to the barn. Thunder still needed to be brushed down and the horses fed. He hadn't missed the empty feed troughs, which also meant the stalls hadn't been cleaned. Mucking stalls was Derek's least favorite chore, and if he didn't straighten up soon, he would be doing it a whole lot more.

Out of the corner of his eye, he spotted the hunched over figure of a boy creeping along the side of the shed, trying to stay low and remain undetected in between the bushes.

Dylan's stomach uncurled a notch.

His brother was okay.

But it also meant it was time to put on his parenting suit. He loved his little brother, but he hated having to become the bad guy, the rule enforcer, the tough big brother. And Derek fought him every inch of the way. Parenting was hard, but unlike his brother, he didn't shirk his responsibilities.

Dylan walked around to the back of the shed. "You can come out of hiding. I've already seen you."

"So what?" Derek grumbled. He crawled out from behind the bush and stood there, his head hung low as if something important were going on down in ant world.

Dylan noticed a splash of red on the side of his cheek. He reached out to grab Derek's chin and pulled his head up for a better look. The gash on his cheek didn't look like a run-in with the pitchfork. Neither did the purpling bruise beginning to form under his eye.

"You been fighting again?" He already knew the answer. He needed to push Kayla to the recesses of his brain and turn his full focus on his brother.

"No." Derek pulled away. He scuffed his boot a few times against the dirt path, sending a cloud of dust into the air.

"No, what?" Respect. Another uphill climb Dylan wasn't willing to forego.

"No, sir," the boy mumbled.

"Don't lie to me about fighting. I know what a black eye looks like. And you know I'll get a call if this happened at school." The school principal was running out of patience the same way Dylan had been out of patience for years.

Silence.

Derek scuffed his boot against the ground harder.

"We can do this the hard way or my way, take your pick."

The hard way included more chores for fighting and also meant he couldn't ride Jezebel, his mare. Jezebel was Derek's escape from reality. A reality that consisted of hard work and no parents. Not exactly a kid's dream childhood, but on a ranch, everyone had to pull their own weight to make it successful, and Derek was no exception. At least until he was old enough to leave, and he was already making plans for that day.

Dylan could relate.

At eighteen, he'd wanted nothing more than to leave the ranch and ride the rodeo circuit. But that was before tragedy struck and their mother died, altering the course of their lives. Dylan had watched her wither away from depression until she'd finally broken and tried to run, taking his baby brother with her. The accident had left both boys motherless, and it was a miracle his brother survived the crash. From that day forward, Dylan had known his brother had to come first.

Derek looked up at him, uncertainty in his expression.

"Bobby was making fun of me again, and I don't like it. Said I always smelled like sh—"

Dylan raised his hand to stop the words. "Don't say it."

"I didn't. He did."

"You know what I mean. You don't have to repeat it." It's not like he'd been a saint at Derek's age, but it *was* his job to raise the bar.

"Fine. He said I always smell like manure." Derek shoved his hands in his front pockets, his shoulders slumped.

"We live on a ranch. Big deal. He lives in town and probably always smells like froufrou soap. It's what's inside that makes the man."

Derek cracked a smile. "Did you just say froufrou?"

"Yes. Don't let the boys get you in trouble. You need to learn to control your actions. And until you do, you need to take on the extra job of spreading the piled-up manure out across the garden plot. More manure chores to make you smell even more manly."

Derek rolled his eyes and groaned at his sentence. "Do I have to? I'm sick of doing chores."

"It's either manure or no Jezebel. What's it going to be?" He couldn't back down.

"That's a no-brainer. I'll shovel the sh—crap."

Dylan grinned when he heard the automatic correction. "Thanks." There was still hope for his brother.

"What for?" Derek's freckled face peered up at him from beneath the brim of his cowboy hat.

"Telling the truth and accepting responsibility for your actions."

"Whatever." The I-don't-care shrug of Derek's shoulders was not in agreement with the gleam in his eyes. Message received.

Dylan knew he was falling short in the emotional support

department, but he was doing the best he could as the sole provider for his brother. Keeping the ranch afloat and trying to make it successful took all his time and energy, but he did it because he loved Derek and he'd fallen in love with the wide-open rolling meadows he'd once hated. Cattle ranching was his life now, and he was determined to make the ranch successful, determined to make the ranch a better place to live. A place Derek, and maybe even Kayla, would want to call home one day. By choice. It was all about choice.

Chapter Three

As Kayla crossed through the backyard on the way to the barn, she couldn't help but look over at the big oak tree and the tire swing hanging from a thick limb. Home of her tree house. The place where she'd first dared to dream of being a vet. It was also the first place she'd dared to let her feelings for Dylan come to light.

Her parents' love and support had allowed her to chase after her dream, but she knew they'd expected her to end up in Riverbend. But that wasn't the road she wanted to travel. It hadn't been when she and Becky had first plotted and planned their escape from the small town as young girls, and it certainly wasn't in her plan after how things had ended with Dylan.

Kayla would probably have stayed for Dylan, her love more than enough to make up for whatever the city had to offer. But in the end, he'd never given her the choice.

And though Becky's road had never left Riverbend, it was entirely her own fault. Kayla didn't know if Dylan had rejected his son, or if Becky had never told him he was a father, but Kayla knew the truth. Her best friend's words of confirmation had been a death toll to every shred of emotion for the guilty pair.

But Becky had ended up with what Kayla could only long for in the middle of the night with silent tears. Dylan's son.

She stopped to look at the barn and frowned. The place needed a little work.

Understatement. It needed a lot of work. The barn doors hung at an awkward angle. Warped boards pulled nails right out of the frame, leaving large openings across the front of the barn. Cracks riddled the side boards from years of the hot, dry sun beating down on them. The brown stain had long since turned a whitish gray, the boards beyond a simple paint job.

She pulled open the barn door and stepped inside. "Dad," she called, hearing a sound from the direction of the hayloft.

"Kayla? Up here." His weathered face poked over the side of the loft with a huge smile.

"Hey, Dad." Joy filled her heart. "I got in a little bit ago."

Lou Anderson climbed down with ease and pulled her into a bear hug, lifting her right off the ground. She didn't care his denim overalls were dusty. She only cared about the love she felt in his embrace.

"You're a sight for sore eyes, child. Glad to have you home."

"Thanks. It's only for a week, but there's plenty of time to get caught up after the wedding."

"You don't come home often enough. I'll be glad when you come home to stay, and this schooling business is behind you." It was the same thing he'd been telling her for years.

He was right, at least about the visiting home part. One more year of school, and she'd be done. She'd have long hours at the clinic, but nothing like the schedule she pulled now, and getting home more often would be possible. They would still only be visits, but perhaps it would smooth over the disappointment of her not moving back. That is, if she survived this visit and seeing him again.

"You know how hard it is with school and clinic hours."

"I know. I know. Can't blame a man for trying to get his daughter to come home." He grinned. "I take it you saw your mother up at the house." He reached up to brush her cheek, his gentle smile at odds with the gruff, hard-work-never-killed-anybody front he presented to the world. His skin weathered and lined like the barn boards from years and years in the sun, working the fields, but his heart hadn't changed. It was still the size of Texas.

She looked at him in question.

"Chocolate." He smiled. "Some things never change."

"Very funny. Yes, I saw her and managed to snag a few Elephant Ears. I can't find anything like hers in Houston. She really ought to patent the recipe, or at least start sending me care packages."

"I think she's holding out for you to come home to get your fill. I thought once you transferred to that fancy vet school of yours in Houston, you'd find more time to visit. Your mother's real lonely without you."

Tag-team guilt. Her mom and dad knew exactly how to apply pressure. And it worked. There wasn't a day that went by she didn't think of home. And there wasn't a day that went by where she didn't think about leaving her parents to manage the farm alone.

"I'm studying to be a small-animal vet, and I am a city girl now, Dad." She smiled to soften the blow, but the words came out all wrong, judging by the tight lines on her dad's face. She hadn't meant to go down this road yet, but unfortunately, she'd been thrown in the middle of it.

"That's where you're wrong, sweetheart. And people in Riverbend do have cats and dogs. What you choose to do with your life is your own decision, but it doesn't change the fact you were born to be the next generation of Andersons to own this place." His voice held a note of finality.

Two completely different lives, but only one could be her future. Riverbend already had a small-animal vet, and the town wasn't big enough for two, but it wouldn't do any good to argue with her dad. She'd made her choice. The clinic where she was working had offered her a partnership when she graduated, and she'd accepted. The only thing left was to tell her parents.

Besides, if she lived in Riverbend, she'd be faced with Dylan and his son on a regular basis. They were living reminders of the heartache and pain she would rather forget. She was over Dylan, but she wasn't so sure she'd ever get over the heartache of losing their son.

"Did you happen to see Dylan at the house? I need his help for a minute," her dad asked.

Kayla tensed.

"He left to check on Derek. He said he'll be back soon. I was hoping we could go for a ride."

Her dad glanced up at the hayloft. "Well, I don't know. There's a lot to be done," he said hesitantly before stepping away from the ladder. "But I reckon I should go with you since you just got here and I wouldn't want you to ride alone."

"I'll help you with the loft tonight in return. Deal?" she asked.

"Deal. Saddle up, and let's get a move on. Day's a wasting."

She'd missed riding Dizzy. Long rides with her steadfast mare were the one source of entertainment she could count on while growing up, and at times, it was the only thing in her past that helped maintain her sanity. Hours and hours at a time, they'd ridden out, discovering every inch of the farm while she poured her heart out to the mare.

It had been a long time since she'd ridden, and it was one of the things she missed most about home. The riding stables outside the city didn't offer her the kind of freedom she had here, and no other horse could ever replace Dizzy.

A few minutes later, saddled up and ready to go, Kayla swung herself up into the saddle. Her dad came over to check the cinches, the same way he'd done when she was a little girl.

"They're tight. I remember how to do it."

"Doesn't matter. A man likes to recheck everything for the safety of his loved ones."

"Well, in that case, check away." She smiled. Independence had its place, but so did love. And right now, she was feeling the love.

They rode out toward the fields, and she looked around, soaking up the hot afternoon sun.

"What did you mean about the boys finishing the rest of the barn tomorrow?" she asked when they slowed to an easy pace, side by side.

"Dylan, Randy, Tommy, and Ethan are coming over to fix up the barn for the ceremony."

She knew the wedding was Saturday afternoon, and the barn had to be cleaned and decorated, but she was surprised to find out who would be doing the work. So much for trying to keep Dylan away from the farm. He must have had a good laugh knowing the plans.

"I heard about Casey. I don't understand why no one told me. I would have come home for his funeral."

"Sweetheart, you were right in the middle of finals and testing for admission to vet school. You were working so hard to get in, and we didn't want to stress you out."

"It still would have been nice to know." Everything he said was true, but it didn't change anything. "I'm sure it was a huge blow to everyone in town."

"It was. The hardest part was they never recovered his body. They were caught behind enemy lines and lost a lot of men that day. Until they recover the bodies, they're considered presumed dead MIA. There was a nice memorial service, but it's been hard for his family to find closure."

"I hadn't heard that part. How awful."

"No one talks about it much. There's been a lot happening around here, and everyone's struggling with the drought. We planned on telling you in person. I'm sorry." He turned his horse toward the southwest fields, and she nudged Dizzy to follow.

"I noticed the place needs some work."

"Yeah, it does." His clipped words were not the elaboration she was looking for.

"Are the crops doing better this year?"

"Nope. In fact, they're worse. What sprinkling of rain we've had hits the hard-packed ground and runs right into the Trinity river. Farmers are the worse hit, but the ranchers aren't doing so well, either. Folks are having to make do the best they can."

"So how are you and Mom doing? I mean, three years in a row, it's got to be tough."

"We're managing with Dylan's help. He's a good man. Built his ranch up right nice. I reckon it's only a matter of time before he finds himself a good, strong woman to love and share his life. And it wouldn't hurt for Derek to have a mother to look after him." He cast her a long look.

His message was about as subtle as getting bucked off a horse. First her mother, and now her father. What on earth would lead them to believe she would be interested in Dylan after all these years? She wasn't a kid anymore, and her mother knew just enough that it should have nixed any thoughts of her and Dylan as a couple.

"Why's he helping out if he's so busy? Surely you could hire someone else. Or does he need the extra income to keep things running?"

Her dad looked at her with a funny expression on his face. "He just helps out. Things have been tough. Money's tight, and he helps any way he can. It's been real nice, like having a son around."

"Lovely." She didn't mean to sound so facetious, but there was no other way for it to be taken. *Dylan, the paragon of virtue. Not.*

"I expect you to be nice to him. I don't rightly know what happened between the two of you, but your mother said some mumbo jumbo about you two being in different places in life. Seeing as you were only eighteen at the time, I think it was probably best for you. Wouldn't have been right for you to give up your dream of becoming a vet."

He was wrong. The best thing for her would have been to stay right here in Riverbend. Maybe then she wouldn't have lost the baby. The doctors didn't have an explanation for her miscarriage, and she would never know the truth, but she did wonder if she was partly to blame. Guilt on top of guilt.

"Wow, is nothing a secret around here?" Kayla turned away, hoping his all-knowing gaze wouldn't see her pain.

One word about the baby, and their attitude toward Dylan would change faster than a burned-out shooting star. Self-preservation kept her quiet. The thought of hurting Dylan paled in comparison to the hurt she'd already suffered.

"I'm also smart enough to figure out it must have had something to do with Becky because you dropped her like a cow drops a calf. And it all happened around the same time. But here's what I do know. I need him. So I'm asking you to be civil."

She closed her eyes and inhaled deeply. Her throat muscles cramped, almost choking her. She reached out to steady herself by holding on to Dizzy's long neck and mane.

"For you, I'd do almost anything." She spurred her horse forward toward the cornfields and left her dad to follow.

Ten minutes later, she slowed the horse, pulling back on the reins. "Whoa, girl," she said softly. She glanced around while she waited for her dad to catch up.

Pathetic.

There was no other way to describe the corn crop. Row after row, the fields were infinitely worse than she imagined. Short and wiry corn stalks with leaves that drooped toward the dry and dusty ground. Four-inch ears of corn with brown dried silk hanging from the top. They should have been twice that size this time of year. The ground was littered with cracks desperate for water to fill the gaps.

"Is everything this bad?" she asked when her father pulled up next to her, a grim look on his face.

"Unfortunately, yes. The drought has taken a toll on everyone around here. Most farms and ranches can weather through one or two years, but three is tough. There's a lot of folks losing farms that have been in their families for generations, just like ours."

"Are we okay?" she asked. This explained why nothing was being fixed up.

"It's been tough for sure. But we're finding ways to keep it going."

"Such as?" She pressed for more information, more concerned about her parents and the homestead than she had been when she arrived and first discovered the deteriorating condition of the farm.

"There's no need for you to worry," he answered.

An evasive answer at best, one that left her wondering what he was trying to hide.

"Dead crops mean no income and no way for you to pay the bills. I'm not a child anymore. I understand the economics of a farm."

"Well, unless you're offering to come home for good and use some of your newfound knowledge to manage the farm, it's nothing for you to worry about." Her dad tapped his heels to the horse's belly and cantered off, not bothering to wait for her reply.

Chapter Four

Dylan rolled over and covered his head with the pillow. It was the only way to drown out the screech of the alarm clock reminding him morning came whether he'd slept the night before or not.

Seeing Kayla again had awakened memories of her, of them together in the tree house. Images that kept him awake long into the night.

Physically, she looked the same. Soft waves of flaming red curls hung loosely down her back and framed her face. Curls he'd last seen draped across a pillow as she lay in his arms and professed her love. And of course, the icy-blue eyes cold with contempt after his rejection, eyes that still had the power to cripple him with their intensity.

She had every reason to hate him. His gut clenched.

Walking away had been unforgivable after she'd entrusted him with her body and her heart, even if he'd walked away to save her from making a mistake. Giving up her dreams and choosing a life that could destroy her hadn't been an option as far as he was concerned.

With nothing to offer her except a failing ranch, a rundown home and the thrill of becoming an eighteen-year-old mother to an eight-year-old boy, Dylan had let her go. He would have loved nothing more than to have her stay, but he'd already seen firsthand the destruction caused when unhappiness and loneliness became a way of life.

And nothing had changed. All the reasons he'd walked away still existed. If she ever came home, it had to be because she wanted to, not because he needed her. He refused to trap her into the solitary life on the ranch, not when he had so little to offer. But it didn't stop him from hoping it would happen one day.

Dylan rolled back over and reached out to silence the incessant alarm, hoping to drive away the pain lodged in his chest. It was sunup. And sunup waited for no one.

He crawled out of bed and threw on a pair of jeans before making his way down the hall. It was going to be a long day, especially with the added workload of getting the Anderson barn ready for the wedding.

"Derek, you up?" He pounded on his brother's bedroom door.

"No. Go away," Derek called out, his voice groggy with sleep.

"Coming in," he said right before he entered and proceeded to yank off the bedspread. "Get a move on. We're running behind, and you'll be late."

"You could just let me skip for a change," Derek grumbled.

"No way. We all have jobs to do, and yours is to get an education and help with the ranch."

"I don't feel good. Everyone should be let off the hook when they're sick," he whined.

Dylan reached out to touch his forehead.

"No fever and no vomiting. Nothing wrong with you I

can't cure with a few nasty chores if you don't get your butt moving and go to school." It was the same old routine, but today Dylan's patience levels were running on extra low.

"Whatever. Just go away so I can get dressed." He felt it was safe to leave once Derek kicked back the sheets and rolled over to sit up on the bed.

In the kitchen, he located a couple of bowls and poured Cheerios and milk for breakfast. After popping bread in the toaster, he grabbed two lunch sacks from the fridge. Luckily, he'd made up several lunches ahead of time, so he was off the hook this morning for that time-consuming responsibility.

A sullen Derek slid onto the wooden stool at the kitchen table. He ate in silence, and for once, Dylan let him. Too tired to do the parenting thing, he polished off his breakfast, took the bowl to the sink to rinse it, and emptied the dregs in his coffee cup down the drain. Behind him, the back door slammed shut. Glancing at the counter, he heaved a sigh of relief. His brother had remembered to take his book bag and his lunch for a change.

He glanced back at the window and spotted Derek pedaling his bike down the driveway. "Have a nice day to you, too," Dylan said out loud to an empty room. Silence was better than an argument any day of the week.

He threw some water and his lunch sack into a duffel bag and headed for the truck, hoping it would start this morning. The old truck needed a new starter, and one of these days, he'd make it a priority to fix. Too many other things needed doing to mess with it today.

It was already getting hot outside, and there wasn't a cloud in the sky. Luckily, the truck started on the second try. Dylan drove down the dirt road and turned left at the end toward the Anderson farm.

Easing past the barn, he checked for signs of life. He spotted Lou astride his horse, coming from around the side of the weathered structure.

"Morning." Dylan waved his arm out the window as he inched closer, not wanting to spook the horse.

"Morning. What brings you out here so early?"

"Thought I'd check on the herd."

"Her or the herd?" Lou grinned.

"The herd," he said, unmistakably pronouncing the *D*.

"I'm not an old fool. I know you and which way the wind blows." Lou's lips curled. "I'll tell you this, she won't be coming back to Riverbend, or you, if we don't figure something out." Lou's matter-of-fact tone slid down Dylan's spine.

"Seems to me a grown woman needs to make her own choices, no matter whether I agree or not. Besides, you and I have a deal not to interfere."

Being a rancher's wife would be a hard life, and it was a life Kayla had already run from once. There was no way in hell he wanted to influence any decision she made to stay or go.

"Well, if that's your attitude, then you're not the man I thought you were. I know the only reason you would have agreed to the Kayla clause would be because you care about her. I'm not blind. Why else would you risk losing the farm and the river rights unless you cared?"

"She has to come home because this is where she wants to be."

"Seems to me, a man who cares for my daughter the way he should, would fight for her," Lou grumbled. The look he shot Dylan's way was as pointed as his words.

"It has to be her choice. Look at Derek. I've tried and tried. Nothing. I can't get through to him because he doesn't want to listen."

"Then I suggest you give up and go check on the herd, because soon them cows is the only thing gonna keep you company. The boy and the woman will move on if you don't fight for them."

Dylan shook his head side to side. "Later, Lou." He lifted his hand in farewell and drove away.

. . .

Kayla stood by the window and looked down into the barnyard. She spotted Dylan's old Ford and pushed the curtain back for a better view.

She would love to be a fly on the barn wall and to hear exactly what they were discussing. Dylan had a way of showing up in person or in conversations more frequently than Kayla would have considered necessary. Considering their history, she found his closeness with her father irritating.

Her father should be talking to her instead. Animal Science wasn't the only thing she'd learned in school, and she could help her dad, if he'd let her. But he wasn't saying a whole lot about the drought situation or the farm, leaving her in the dark each time she asked.

Families were losing land passed from one generation to the next and being forced to uproot and relocate because of the drought. It would devastate her father to lose the only home he'd ever known, but Kayla had no way of knowing where he stood. Years ago, he'd taken out a loan to cover the shortfall between her scholarship and her school bill, and it was the loan she was worried about now. If he lost the farm, it would be her fault.

The farm should have been hers one day, but she'd walked away with no intentions of returning. Nothing had changed, but it didn't mean she could stand by and do nothing. No matter what, she owed it to her parents to make sure they could live out their lives where her dad grew up, and in the only home where he would ever be happy.

And she had a pretty good idea how to make it happen. An irrigation system with a pump would be costly, but it was the perfect plan to save the farm. She just needed to get her father to agree to let her help.

Kayla stifled a yawn. Her body ached in places she hadn't used in years, and it kept her awake long into the night. She'd forgotten how physically demanding it was to pitch hay and ride a horse.

Dylan drove down the dirt road that led toward the back of their property and toward the river. "Hmmm." She tapped a finger against her chin. Where would he be going? And more importantly, why? Based on what her father told her, he ought to have enough work on his own property to keep him busy without sticking his nose into her family business.

It wasn't long before she was dressed, out the door, and on her way to the barn, grateful she hadn't run into anyone along the way. There was no way she wanted to explain where she was headed. Within minutes, she'd saddled Dizzy and was headed in the direction Dylan had taken.

Kayla followed the road looking around for signs of him or the truck.

Coming over the crest of a hill, she spotted him down by the river.

She slowed the mare, staying hidden behind a grove of trees and bushes. "Whoa, girl," she said softly, tying the reins to a tree.

Edging closer, she peered between the bushes to spy on Dylan, shocked to see a large herd of cattle grazing in the open pasture next to the river, many of them belly deep in the slow-moving water. Her dad hadn't brought her out this way yesterday, and he certainly hadn't mentioned owning cattle.

A quick tally showed close to three hundred head, which was no small potatoes in Riverbend, especially given the overall acreage of the farm. It would have cost him a fortune to bring in a herd this size, and from what she could tell, money was in short supply. As a business plan, it wasn't a good time to get into ranching. The drought would have driven up the price of cattle, not to mention the feed.

The initial cost alone would have been enormous, but the upkeep and labor a herd this size would require would never work for the small outfit her dad ran. It hurt he hadn't bothered to consult her before making such a huge decision. She may have left to pursue her dreams, but that didn't mean she didn't care about them or the family farm. Far from it.

Her dad's reasoning for buying the cattle didn't matter. What was done was done. Plan A to save the farm wasn't an option if there was a herd of cattle to keep fed and watered, but she was determined to figure out a Plan B.

Dylan leaned down to scoop water from the river into a small container. Sitting back on his haunches, he held up a vial, poured some of the river water into the tube, and shook it gently. Water testing was common practice when herds relied on ground water sources, and with water being scarce around here she was sure ranchers and farmers alike were highly protective of the Trinity River. The question remained, however, why was Dylan doing it?

Dizzy whinnied from behind. "Shhhh. Easy, girl. Let's not advertise we're here." She stroked the horse's long neck and mane to comfort her. Kayla turned back to watch Dylan but couldn't see him. She scanned the area. Nothing.

Damn. Where did he go? Maybe he was behind the truck and out of sight.

"Morning, Kayla. What brings you out here so early?"

"Ahhhh." She spun around to face him. His voice had been casual, but he'd scared the bejeebers out of her. *Damn him.*

There was no use pretending she hadn't been caught spying. Humor was her next best defense. The girl who got hurt and had run away had long since grown up and didn't shirk from anyone. Least of all Dylan.

"Ummm, just out for a morning ride and stopped to let the horse rest." It sounded good.

"Try again," he said, his lips twitching in a half-hearted smile.

"The horse wandered out here, tied herself to the tree, and I had to come find her?" She could play this game if he wanted, but she had no intention of admitting the truth.

"I remember plenty of times I caught you spying on me and the guys when you used to follow us around like a little pest. Apparently, spying is another quality of yours that remains unchanged."

What did he mean by another quality? Spying had worked wonders when she was younger, and she saw no reason not to continue if it got her the truth. There were quite a few truths she'd learned in her teenage years following the Fearless Five around like a little sister.

"Who said I was spying? Can't I stop and rest my horse while I'm out for a ride?"

"Your daddy may have believed you back when you were younger, but I never fell for your stories. There's no reason you can't tell me the truth. We were friends once. Close friends, if I remember," he added, stepping in closer.

He reached a hand toward her face. She froze, her brain not capable of functioning. She held her breath and remembered the last time his hand had reached out to touch her, his lips not far behind. Her body remembered his touch and had a mind of its own, eliminating any will power she needed to stop him. Tingles raced down her spine, short, shallow breaths came faster even as time slowed to a brief halt.

He plucked a leaf out of her hair. "A leftover from your hiding place," he said, his voice husky.

She wasn't the only one remembering another time and place.

Kayla let out the deep breath she'd been holding. In relief or disappointment, she wasn't sure. Memory lane was best left in the dark corners of her mind and forgotten. Older and wiser, there was no way she would fall for his charm a second time around.

It was better to get straight to the point.

"What do you do for my father? And when did he get cattle? By the looks of things, there's a lot not getting done around here, and yet suddenly he has a herd of cows."

The smile slipped from his face. "You're stepping in a cow patty on this one. You might want to ask him instead."

"He's not answering, so I'm asking you. My father's not a cattle rancher, and you and I both know it."

"He's doing the best he can with the drought. Not that you'd understand, because you don't come around much. And for your information, the herd is mine." Dylan's brown eyes bored into her with hawk-like precision.

The only thing he'd see was relief. Relief she could go back to Plan A and the irrigation system and not have to deal with a herd of oversize beasts.

"Yours? How do you have this many head of cattle when your dad never ran more than a hundred?" Not that she cared. The only thing she cared about was the cattle didn't belong to her parents. They were Dylan's, and the result as far as she was concerned was the same. They had to go.

"Not that it's any of your business, but I'm sure you recall my father died. There was an insurance policy, and I used the money to make something of the ranch. To make a home for Derek and…"

"And?"

"Never mind. It doesn't matter." She knew the hard look on his face. Whatever he'd been about to say would remain unspoken.

"If they're your cattle, why are they on our land?"

"Because they need the water. It's cheaper than me having it transported in every day for a herd this size. The reservoirs on my ranch dried up earlier this spring."

Kayla pulled her hair into a ponytail and rubbed the back of her neck before letting the hair tumble back into place. "But our crop is failing. Why isn't my dad having the water pumped up to the fields? Surely he can afford to put in irrigation with what you're paying to lease the grazing land and river."

"The laws are clear about ground water rights during a drought. The land comes with priority licensing rights to the water, and there are limits on how much can be diverted. The water rights with this property are only enough to cover the herd."

Listening to Dylan was an eye opener. He was always on top of things, but the calm confidence he exuded was mind boggling. But it didn't change a thing. Her father's homestead was more important, and it was up to her to set the record straight.

"But it's his land. If he doesn't save this crop, he might be flat broke and could lose the farm like so many of our neighbors. Don't you care?"

"Of course, I care. And I'm doing what I can to help."

Kayla disagreed, her temper escalating. In fact, Dylan appeared to be a part of the problem. A big part.

"By taking his water allotment for your cows? I don't think so. I don't know how you talked him into this, but I'll make him see sense. You managed to make a gullible young woman believe you cared, but once you got what you wanted, you walked away. I'll be damned if I'll let you destroy my father the same way you did me."

Dylan cringed as she delivered the scathing blow. Finally,

the words came when she needed them. And they felt good. *Damn good.*

She stepped in close to Dizzy, placed her foot in the stirrup, and pulled herself up into the saddle.

"You'd better make sure those cows drink plenty of water this weekend, because by Monday, they better be gone. Consider my verbal warning as notice served."

Chapter Five

Kayla glanced at her watch. An hour had passed since she'd fled from her encounter with Dylan, and still he was foremost in her brain, not banished as she would have liked. She didn't see anyone around as she approached the barn and slid out of the saddle. Her legs rebelled against the change, almost crumpling beneath her weight like wet noodles. Sweat glistened from Dizzy's velvety coat. Kayla could relate and would give anything for a shower, but that would have to wait until she finished grooming the horse.

It had been amazing to be back in the saddle, the wind rushing through her hair, the steady beat of the horse's hooves pounding the ground. She pressed her face against the mare's long, sleek neck.

Aside from her anger with Dylan, the ride this morning had been fun. Different than when she was a young girl. Back then, she'd been more caught up in the image of a good-looking cowboy in tight-fitting blue jeans than she was in the beauty of the land. Of noticing the birds, or the lizards, or even the deer she spotted off in the distance. Today had certainly been an eye-opener. The quiet beauty of the morning had drawn her in and away from the hustle and bustle of the city and its tiring pace.

Dizzy was getting older and would have to be retired soon, but Kayla loved her all the same, maybe more. Her appreciation of the mare's steadfast qualities and loyalty were more profound now than before she'd left home. Dizzy had been a handful as a young foal, dancing herself in circles when anything new caught her eye, earning her name honestly. But to Kayla, she was perfect.

She grabbed an apple from the basket closest to Dizzy's stall and fed it to the mare. She picked up the grooming brush and began a rhythmic stroke down the horse's back. Each stroke was a little stronger than the last as everything she tried to forget for the past hour replayed in her head. Anger simmered deep within.

Dylan had no right to put her father in a position to lose the farm that had been in their family for generations. And it was up to Kayla to help save the homestead. Come Monday, she'd start to put Plan A into place, hopefully with her father's blessing.

"That was great. Don't tell anyone, old girl, but I miss riding. More than I could imagine. And I miss you." The horse nuzzled her shoulder in response.

Unfortunately, she'd be gone long before the soft bruising aches settling in her legs went away. Somehow, she'd find a way to visit more often when she graduated. Life couldn't be all work, and she needed to pay closer attention to her parents' affairs.

"I'm sorry I left and didn't come back much, girl. But I heard Mom rides you sometimes, so I know you get good exercise." Kayla gently swatted the horse's flank, followed by a slow rub.

Chats with Dizzy weren't unusual, and if horses could

talk, Kayla would be in big trouble. Time after time, Becky had been stuck in town helping her mother, leaving Kayla to pour her heart out to the only set of ears who would listen without judgment. Dizzy had been the perfect listener. Always had been, always would be.

A sound alerted Kayla she wasn't alone. She looked around and tried to pinpoint the location. She knew every inch of the barn and every nook of the hundred-acre farm.

Her gaze zeroed in toward the back corner. It was probably a cat, preferably not a rat. There it was again. *Bigger than a cat or a rat.*

"Is someone in here?" she called out, taking a few steps toward the storage shed against the back wall. She lifted the wooden lever and pulled the door open slowly. Of all the things that crossed her mind, a kid wasn't one of them. Especially not one who looked like a miniature replica of Dylan.

She hadn't seen the kid since he was eight years old and here he was, huddled on the floor in the corner of the tack room, and if she had to take a guess, hiding.

"Derek?" she asked, keeping her voice low. The fear in his eyes was already enough to make her want to hug away his worries.

"Who are you?" he asked, not bothering to answer her question.

His tone was defensive and challenging, more so than she would have expected from a thirteen-year-old. It took her by surprise, but then she didn't have much experience with kids.

"I'm Kayla Anderson. I know you must be Derek." A fleeting glimpse of recognition flashed across his face.

"You're the spitting image of your brother," she added when he remained silent.

Derek's shoulders pulled tighter together, his eyes darting toward the opening behind her. It wouldn't take much for the kid to bolt. He was angry at something or someone, and the chip on his shoulder looked greater than he could handle alone. The need to help tugged at her heartstrings.

"Lucky me," he muttered.

Kayla chose to ignore his comment, for now anyway. It was better to start with a more obvious and easier question. "Shouldn't you be in school?"

"No. I'm sick, but my jerk of a brother wouldn't let me stay home." *Ouch.* Dylan *was* a jerk, but to hear Derek call him one didn't bode well for the direction of this conversation. Helping the kid was one thing, helping him deal with Dylan would be borderline insanity, not to mention impossible.

"You don't look sick. I was a kid once, too. There were plenty of days I wanted to skip out of school, and I always thought I had good reasons. But luckily, I didn't, because without an education, I wouldn't have anything."

It sounded like the perfect parent response. Maybe Derek couldn't see beyond the chores and the ranch yet, but soon enough, whether to stay or go would be his choice. He'd have the chance to follow his dreams, but he needed to be prepared.

Kayla offered her hand to help him up. He ignored it, pushing himself off the ground to stand.

"You want to tell me what's going on? Issues at school or issues with Dylan. Which is it?" She squashed any thought of repercussions from Dylan. Maybe he didn't even have to find out she was meddling.

"None of your business." Head hung down and hands shoved in his pockets, he scuffed his feet, kicking at the hay strewn across the floor.

He was thirteen. And a boy. She didn't expect it to be easy, but she wasn't giving up, not yet anyway. Perhaps a little incentive would help. Kid style.

"I've got an Elephant Ear covered with chocolate and

bananas up at the house that says you could make it my business." Dylan's comment yesterday about the pastries almost guaranteed her a win for this round. Besides, having missed breakfast when she rode out earlier, a loaded pastry sounded pretty darn good.

"You ain't gonna rat me out, are you?" A light of interest sparked on his face.

"Depends if we talk or if you keep shutting me out. I don't see any reason to bring either your brother or the school screaming down your back. But that doesn't mean I'm going to turn my head the other way. It's either me, the school, or your brother. Take your pick."

"Are you serious?" His body stilled. She had his full attention at least for the moment.

"An Elephant Ear and a glass of milk serious." *Bribery at its finest.* Kayla waited while he weighed his options.

"It don't matter anyway, so deal. It's not like the school won't tell Dylan."

"Good choice. But if you want privacy, I suggest you start talking. Once we get to the house, it's all bets off, because my mother will be there. She may not see things the way I do."

"You're different," he said, biting the inside of his cheek. Proof he wasn't as tough inside as the hostile, bad-boy attitude he was trying hard to project.

Poor kid had been through a lot, losing his parents when he was only a little kid, and then to be stuck with Dylan as a father substitute. If his behavior was a cry for help, there was no way she would walk away. That was Dylan's mode of operation, not hers.

"I hope that's a good thing." She laughed.

"You promise not to tell Dylan?"

"I promise." He had no idea how easy it was to agree. Talking to Dylan wasn't on her list of priorities, and the promise had a bonus. Derek's confidence.

"Unless you're in danger," she added quickly. There was no way she could *not* tell Dylan if the kid was in real trouble.

"Only the danger of being laughed out of school and dying from boredom." It was a start. His answer didn't explain what was wrong, but it did set her mind at ease.

Kayla let out a deep breath. She could do this. After all, she'd been a kid once. Ironically, it was Dylan who had guided her through the messy part of life called childhood. Why he wasn't having the same sort of conversations with Derek, she didn't have a clue.

"Okay." She turned toward the barn door and took a few steps, hoping he would follow.

"That's it? You're not gonna ask me tons of questions to find out why?"

She turned back to face him.

"I'm here to listen, not pry."

"I get it. Why would you? It's not like you know me or anything, so why should you care?" He held his body stiff and unyielding, as if somehow it would ward off the unwanted pain of rejection.

Time to call his bluff. She leveled him with a determined gaze. "Confidences are about a willingness to share. If I need to drag it out of you, it's not a confidence. If you want to tell me, you will. And you still get the Elephant Ears." She smiled, trying to put him at ease. "Coming?" She didn't wait for his answer and turned to walked away. Kayla held her breath. Hoping.

And then she heard it. The scuff of a boot behind her, then another.

She pulled the door open and let him pass through before securely latching it closed.

"I hate it here. It's always school and work, school and work. There're no kids nearby, and the kids at school hate me," he grumbled as they fell in step, side by side.

Now we're getting somewhere.

She suspected he hated chores and the boredom. She could relate from her own past. The kids at school hated him, well, that part, she was wading in deep, uncharted waters.

"And my broth...hates..." Derek's voice was barely a whisper as he choked the words out. Low enough she almost had to ask him to repeat them, but her brain filled in what she missed.

"Derek, listen to me." She stopped to get his undivided attention. "You're wrong. Please don't ever think that way. I may be four years younger than your brother, but I was old enough to watch him take care of you like you were his own son."

She meant every word. Dylan had given up his own dreams when his mother died, and any hope of ever leaving vanished when his father passed away a few years later.

Dylan was the most responsible, selfless person she knew. Except when it came to her. But his feelings toward her were irrelevant at the moment. However, it was important for Derek to get a glimpse of understanding about the sacrifices Dylan had made, all for him. Judging by the scowl on Derek's face, understanding was not one of the emotions he was feeling.

She had to try again. "He loves you. Everything he's done to hold the ranch together has been for you, to give you a home. He had to take on a ton of responsibility after your parents died, and he did it without a second thought for his own dreams."

Mentioning his parents probably wasn't the smartest thing she could have done. A flash of pain flittered across his face, but luckily, it disappeared just as quickly, and in its place, a sudden inquisitive interest took root.

"What do you mean?"

"Dylan wanted to be a rodeo star. He dreamed of getting

out of Riverbend and making it big. Anything but ranching. And chores. And boredom. Sound familiar?"

Just like it had once been her and Becky's dream to leave. Only Becky had never escaped.

Poor choices had a way of stealing your dreams, and sleeping with the guy your best friend loved qualified as a poor choice.

And still, Kayla would have given up everything she'd done in the last five years to change places with Becky, because somehow, Becky was the one who ended up with what Kayla wanted desperately and lost. Dylan's son.

Becky had never told anyone the identity of the father of her child, but Kayla knew the gut-wrenching truth. Had seen it with her own eyes and had it confirmed by Becky. It didn't get any more real.

"He's never said anything to me about it," he mumbled.

She tried to close the door on memory lane and focus on Derek.

"Maybe because it's not important to him now. You are."

"He sure don't show it." Derek continued to keep pace next to her as they neared the house.

"What do you mean?" she asked.

"He doesn't have time for me. Any idea what it's like to be the only kid who doesn't have parents come to school stuff, the only kid who can't go to town to the soda shop and hang? Dylan's always got an excuse, and I've always got chores. And when you muck stalls every night, it's kinda hard to get rid of the smell. The kids laugh and tease me about the way I stink." It was the most he'd talked since she'd found him in the shed, and it was enlightening.

"I'm sorry. Kids can be hard on other kids, and unfortunately, we can't fix them. But you can work on fixing what ails you."

Derek stepped in front of her and stopped, and Kayla ran

into the slender boy, almost knocking him down. She put out her hand to steady them both.

"What do you mean?" he asked.

"For starters, ignore the kids. They'll grow up someday, and they won't be half the person you are if you learn how to be nice to people and treat them the way you want to be treated. I'm sure it's hard to turn the other cheek, but the bigger man who does is the one who wins the fight in the long run."

"You sound like Dylan." It didn't come out as a compliment.

"Maybe Dylan's right." It pained her to say the words. "And your brother has his hands full doing the job of two parents. Maybe you could cut him some slack. Do you usually see both parents of every kid at school events?"

"No."

"Want to know why? The other parent is at work. And Dylan's doing the work of two, which doesn't leave him much time. I'm sure he'd love to be at your events, but then who would cover his other jobs? When you wear the mom, dad, and ranch manager hats, the work is never done."

Defending Dylan didn't come easy, but it was for Derek. And it wasn't the kid's fault Dylan was still a jerk.

"How come you're so smart?" he asked.

Gotcha. The full circle. "Because I stayed in school and paid attention."

"Figures you'd say that. Are we done yet?" Derek grinned. Her heart did a little flip.

"No. There's one other thing." She stopped short of the house to finish the conversation. Several trucks were parked out front, which meant the wedding cavalry had arrived to work on the barn. She hoped Dylan wasn't a part of the group, for her and Derek's sake.

"You're bored. I remember the feeling well, trust me.

What interests you? What have you always wanted but don't have? Sometimes you have to dream small before you can realize the big dreams you want to go after."

"I have Jezebel, but I can't ride out far because I'm too young and everyone's always too busy to go with me. I like dogs, but Dylan says they're too much trouble and he can't take on more. I wouldn't mind trying bull riding, but they tell me I'm too small at school."

Kayla had to agree with the riding restrictions. The dog, well, that would be a perfect idea, but Kayla knew getting Dylan to change his mind would be next to impossible, given his history with dogs. But the bull riding, surely if Dylan knew he was interested it would help to forge a bond between the two brothers.

"Bull hockey," she said. "If you're smaller, you just need to hang on tighter. Have you told Dylan?"

"Nah. He don't care what I want, only that I get my chores done," he said.

"Give him a chance, you might be surprised. Your brother has some slick moves he could teach you."

Derek's face lit up at the prospect. "Really?"

"Really."

"Cool. Um. Sure. I'll think about it." Back to thirteen going on eighteen.

The front porch screen door creaked open.

"Hey, Randy. Come and look at what the cows called home from the city. If it isn't little pesky Kayla Anderson." Tommy looked great, and still every bit a cowboy, his grin wider than the brim of his hat. He stepped off the porch and wrapped her in a big bear hug.

"Hey to you, too." She laughed. "Put me down, you big buffoon, you're killing me."

No sooner than her feet touched the ground, she was lifted back into the air for another embrace. "Little Kayla's not so little anymore. Quite the sight for this cowboy's eyes," Randy said with a wink.

"Nonsense. Flattering me won't get you what half the women in the county probably throw at you willingly," she teased.

Randy was always the big flirt, and women ate it up.

Derek had stepped off to the side, looking unsure of himself. Her heart went out to the kid. A boy trying to find his way into a man's world.

"How come you ain't in school, Derek?" Tommy asked.

"He's not feeling well, and I'm keeping an eye on him." She'd jumped in without thought, but Derek's smile of approval was worth the little white lie. Without a friend, Kayla would have been lost growing up on the outskirts of town. She wouldn't be here long enough to change anything long term, but for now, she could be his friend, and that included helping him out of a tough spot.

"Good thing. Dylan would skin him alive if he was cutting school again," Randy said.

"Well, he's not. And we were just going inside for milk and Elephant Ears, if there're any left after the two of you beat us to the kitchen. Care to join us?"

"Would love to catch up with you, but we're here to clean the barn for the wedding. Maybe later, darling. Good to see you again," Tommy said.

"And if you're not too city soft, you could always pitch in. Would make the work go easier if we had a sweet thing looking like you do working with us." Still the charmer.

The two men raised a hand in farewell and shuffled off toward the barn. "Later," they called out.

She pulled Derek into the house and made her way to the kitchen. "Come on, let's go see if they left us any chocolate and banana toppings for our Ears."

"Sounds good." He grinned as they entered the house.

"What the hell are you doing here when you should be in school?" Dylan's large frame filled the doorway, his voice hard and unyielding as he stared down at his little brother and waited for an answer.

Derek's happy laughter disintegrated. Minutes ago, she'd promised herself she'd do what she could for Derek while she was here, and although it was one thing to lie to the others, lying to Dylan's face was a lot harder.

And it shouldn't be. Years ago, she'd gone all out to break through the wall he'd built between them, and when he'd finally succumbed, she'd thought they would be together forever. That he was her destiny.

She'd been so naive. Dylan had only wanted another notch on his belt. Lying to him now shouldn't mean a damn thing.

"He stopped here on his way to school because he wasn't feeling well. I told him to stay until he felt better." The lie rolled right off her tongue without a glitch.

"Since when do you have the right to interfere?"

Kayla knew he wouldn't appreciate her help, but it was too bad. The boy needed a champion, and for the next week, he'd found one. "You weren't around. For heaven's sake, get over yourself. It's just one day."

"One day of many. Something you wouldn't know anything about since you never come around."

"Well, maybe you don't know everything, either." Dylan's jaw would have hit the floor if it was possible.

Point for me.

"What's that supposed to mean?" Dylan demanded, stepping closer.

Derek's eyes widened in alarm. He would never trust her if she failed him now.

"Nothing. It doesn't matter. Nothing matters to you. It didn't before, and it doesn't now." Years of pain echoed in her words, demanding their place in the universe.

Another point for me.

Dylan's expression hardened. "Is this about Derek, or about you and me?" The deadly calm of his voice made her nervous.

She swallowed hard, trying to find a way to answer. "Derek. There isn't a you and me." Another lie, but a necessary one.

"That's one point of view," Dylan said, turning to his brother. "What's going on? The truth."

"Um, I told you I didn't feel good this morning, and you didn't believe me. It got worse, so I stopped here, j-just like Kayla said." Derek squirmed under Dylan's gaze.

One eyebrow arched questioningly. "Ms. Anderson to you," Dylan said.

Derek stood a little taller. "She told me to call her Kayla. We're friends."

"Is that a fact?"

Chapter Six

Dylan didn't know how his brother had managed to pull Kayla into his little skip-school game, but he intended to find out. First chance he got, they would need to have a good long chat. But there was something entirely different going on with Kayla, her words loaded with deeper meaning. Finding out what probably wouldn't be as easy as a chat, but he'd find a way.

He wiped at the sweat dripping down his face with the cotton sleeve of his T-shirt, stood up straight, and rolled his shoulders to ease the tightness. They'd moved hay and cleaned the barn for three hours and it probably hadn't looked this good in fifty years.

The barn door creaked open. Dylan stopped to watch Kayla lug in a giant picnic basket. Tommy managed to get to her first, and the pair shared a laugh as he took the basket from her arms and carried it to the table. Dylan stayed partially hidden around the corner but had a clear line of vision to watch her.

She was like a cool drink of water to a man in the desert,

and right about now, the barn was as scorching hot as a desert, without all the sand. But he wasn't complaining if the result was seeing Kayla dressed in short shorts and a skimpy tank top. The image reminded him of the last time he'd seen her exposing almost as much flesh. It was the one and only time he'd lost control, something he couldn't afford to do again.

It had been a day that started like any other day. A day that went completely right and completely wrong in the space of an hour. He'd been a fool to think he could give in to her and walk away without paying a hefty price.

He should have sensed something was different when she called him and asked him to meet her at the tree house. Her voice had been different, but he'd ignored it. The gleam in her eyes had been different, but he'd ignored it. Her innocence at odds with the curiosity of a woman testing her boundaries, but he'd ignored it. He'd thought he could handle it. He'd thought everything was under control.

He'd thought wrong.

Unprepared for her version of show and tell, the minute she'd pulled her T-shirt over her head, he'd known he was in trouble. His brain had said run like hell, but his feet had stood rooted to the spot.

The dark-blue fabric of her lacy bra barely covered her breasts, their smooth, creamy complexion begging him to touch. She'd leaned up against the tree, her long, sexy legs barely covered by cutoff shorts, their frayed edges curled up seductively, beckoning the eye higher to her flat belly button, pierced and bejeweled with a red ruby. God, she'd been a sight to behold.

Bolder than any cowboy he'd ever met, her intense gaze had crippled his ability to think straight. He'd been completely and irrevocably lost the second her top hit the ground. Never again had he been able to see her as a pesky little sister. She was all woman. Sexy. Bold.

Their first kiss had been filled with an awakening fire that burned hotter and hotter, her body melting into his arms, full of trust.

It was only after they'd made love that he'd realized the magnitude of his mistake. Her declaration of love and her determination to stay with him and forsake all her dreams had been a rude reminder of what was at stake.

There was no doubt she'd belonged to him, but there was nothing anyone could do to convince him to let her stay. If she'd stayed, he would have destroyed her.

His dreams had died with the death of his parents, but Kayla's had still been out there, full speed ahead. He hadn't wanted to derail her.

Their magical time together had ended with soul-wrenching finality, but it had been a small price to pay compared to the price his mother had paid for the same mistake.

A shrill whistle broke into memory lane. "Come and get it. Dad, Randy, Tommy, lunch is served," she hollered.

He'd taught her how to whistle like a cowboy. Shrill, long, and loud. She had it down to perfection.

Food was like gold to a cowboy, and it didn't take long for everyone to gather around.

"Where's Dylan?" Randy asked.

About time someone noticed his absence.

"I'm coming. Keep your pants on, cowboy," Dylan said, stepping out from behind the corner stall.

"That's not what my lady friend said last night when—"

"That's enough, Randy. Watch your mouth in front of my daughter." Lou shot Randy a look of warning.

"Sorry, sir. Sorry, Kayla." Served him right for running his mouth. Randy was keen on the ladies, and he hadn't taken his eyes off Kayla since she'd walked through the door. But Randy knew the score. Friends didn't poach in friends' territory, and the Fearless Five were more than friends. They were like brothers. Should count for a whole lot more.

"Sorry, Dylan, I forgot you were here." Kayla said, her apology void of any sincerity. A little too lighthearted, and a little too late.

"Ouch," Tommy said. "Lady knows how to make a man feel special, don't she?" He laughed, grabbing another bottle of water.

"She does at that." Dylan shouldn't have said it, but the temptation was impossible to resist. He was rewarded with a stony gaze meant to kill. She knew exactly what he meant. Luckily, the others didn't.

The conversation switched back to wedding preparations and what still needed to be done before they could call it quits for the night.

"I better get back to the house. Enjoy the rest of your lunch."

"Wait, Kayla," Randy called out. "We need your help."

"Randy's right, honey. None of us have a clue about decorations, and we're all finished with the cleaning part. Can't you stay and order us around? Surely that would appeal to your sense of humor?" Lou tossed out the challenge, knowing Kayla wouldn't refuse. When it came to challenges, Kayla never backed down.

"Okay," she agreed with a grin. "But I'm in charge."

Hour after hour, Kayla directed, and everyone marched to her orders. The place began to look less and less like a barn and more like a fairy tale wedding scene out of a Disney movie.

Balloons and streamers. Tables and chairs. Centerpieces. Flowers. Candles that had no business being in a barn. He hoped no one was foolish enough to light one. And the archway. It was a barn, for Pete's sake. What was wrong with getting married under a barn door instead of hauling in some fancy wrought-iron artwork archway decorated with horses? There were plenty of horses in the barn to add ambience, including the soft whinny of a mare for real music. No metal archway could do that. And no number of scented candles or flowers would change the aroma of manure.

The only bonus of the entire afternoon had been watching Kayla in action. When she deigned to speak to him, it had been to give orders, but it was a start. Five years ago, she'd taken charge and let him know what she wanted, and it seemed like she still had no problem taking charge, only now it was with more confidence.

She possessed an undeniable strength. *Unlike my mother.*

The wayward thought struck him hard, like a hammer to the chest. Kayla was strong without a doubt, but would she have been strong enough? It was a question doomed to remain unanswered.

He turned the corner and didn't see Kayla hunched over in front of Dizzy's stall until all of his six-foot-two frame collided with her slender form, sending her flying. His hands shot out to grab her hips before she landed unceremoniously in a heap on the ground.

"Are you okay? Sorry." His hands lingered longer than necessary, but he couldn't let go. Touching her again was like fire in his veins.

She turned around to say something, her mouth hanging open in surprise, but she didn't say a word.

"Kayla, what is it?" he asked. Her eyes misted, tears threatening to swell and overflow. Night after night, he'd dreamt of holding her again, but this wasn't how he pictured it.

Dylan closed his eyes and dropped his arms. The temptation to kiss her was strong, but he couldn't afford to make another mistake. Sucking in a deep breath to calm his racing heart and hormones, he sensed the exact moment she fled. Her flight would delay the inevitable discussion they would have, but they *would* have it. If nothing else, her reaction was proof nothing between them was over.

. . .

What was she thinking? Kayla tried so hard to ignore everything about Dylan, but her eyes gravitated back to watch him while he worked. Hard, lean muscles flexed like bands of steel across his naked back. The guys had shed their shirts in the stifling heat of the barn, but it was only Dylan's half-naked body causing her trouble. A body she knew intimately and remembered as if it were yesterday.

But a nice butt, bulging pecs, and a swoon-worthy face weren't qualities that meant a damn thing compared to ones like trust, or the true heart of a man.

For one split second she forgot the past. Forgot why she hated him. Forgot everything, except how much she wanted to kiss him again. To feel his mouth pressed against hers. For one split second she'd been the same naïve little girl chasing after him.

Dylan's kiss and touch had promised her the moon, but in the aftermath of making love, his words had dealt her a killing blow topped off with a healthy dose of betrayal. There wasn't a single reason to give him the time of day. Except one. Dylan Hunter still made her feel things she shouldn't. Feelings that should have died after his betrayal. Feelings that should have been dead and buried with their son.

She was positive he wanted to kiss her. She'd seen the same look in his eyes once before. But unlike last time, this time he stopped. And unlike last time, this time she was grateful.

Kayla gathered up all the lunch plates, glasses, and discarded napkins, looking for a quick escape back to the house. Good food and hungry men always made cleanup easy.

The barn door scraped open, and Kayla turned to check out the new arrivals.

"Sophia," she cried out in excitement. She dropped the lunch basket back on the table to hug Sophia. Her cousin's timely entrance was the rescue she needed.

"Oh my gosh. Look at this place. It's beautiful. I knew you'd make it perfect. I've missed you so much." Sophia hugged her tight again. She stepped back to look around with tears in her eyes.

"I'm so glad you agreed to be a part of my special day." Sophia smiled.

"I wouldn't miss it for all the Elephant Ears in Texas. Although couldn't you have found someone other than Ethan? I mean really?" she said, grinning up at the big lug standing next to Sophia, his arm around her possessively. The same big lug Kayla had always considered as a big brother.

"Hey, I resent that, squirt." Ethan ruffled her hair.

"That's saying a lot, because I know how you are with those Elephant Ears. I remember a time you hid three in a shoebox in your bedroom so no one else would get them and then forgot them until a week later. Rock hard and useless." Sophia laughed.

"See, there you have it. And as for you, Ethan, I know you better than most, so don't you forget it.

"I'm sure. You followed us around like a puppy dog and invaded our privacy on more than one occasion. Lord knows how many times we didn't know you were hiding and watching." He winked.

"The stories I could tell. But for now, my lips are sealed. Unless you break Sophia's heart, then I would have to spill my guts. Right down to Mr. Todd's bathroom, er, um, let's call it a prank."

"Kayla. Stop. You know about that?" Shock was etched across Ethan's face as clear as the morning sun on a cloudless day.

"What? You have to tell me." Sophia laughed.

"I know lots of things, so behave, is all I'm saying." The guys had teased her endlessly for years, so it didn't hurt to give back a little now that she could hold her own.

"I promise to love and hold her, in sickness and in health, 'til death do us part," he said, his hand clutching his heart in an exaggerated gesture of affection.

"Save it for the vows tomorrow. Just one of those boys-will-be-boys pranks, Sophia. No worries," she said, sending her cousin a devilish wink.

Doing Jenny Hopkins in the bathroom hadn't exactly been a prank. Kayla had hidden in the broom closet of the bathroom, curious what the two were up to. If she'd have known, she would have made her presence known and left. But it was too late by the time she knew what was happening.

Everything she'd learned that day had changed her attitude toward Dylan. It was the first time she'd ever pictured Dylan doing to her the things she'd heard Jenny and Ethan doing. Things a man and a woman did to each other for pleasure. It was enough to make her want to put an end to Dylan's sisterly treatment, to make him want her as a lover.

The others came over to welcome Sophia and Ethan. Easy laughter, teasing, and honest to goodness, real downhome pleasure, just like old times. How could she have forgotten this part?

The more they talked, the more Kayla noticed she was an outsider looking in. A part of the group and yet apart from the group, and she didn't care much for the feeling.

"Hey, sorry guys. But I need to head up to the house to help Mom get dinner ready while you finish up. Sophia, you coming?"

"Of course. Bye, guys," Sophia said, giving Ethan his own special goodbye kiss.

Her cousin was lucky. She'd found the love of her life, and tomorrow, they would be joined together, happily ever after. She knew it didn't always turn out that way. Lots of her friends and acquaintances back in the city had already been married and divorced, some with kids caught in the middle.

Something she wouldn't ever have to worry about.

The young doctor at the hospital hadn't been able to explain her second trimester miscarriage, and he hadn't been very reassuring about her future ability to have a baby safely. But his words had been enough to make her steer clear of even thinking of trying to have a baby. There was no way she could go through the heartache of another miscarriage, and the risk was too great.

Her father had taught her the difference between needing and wanting, a lesson she'd been forced to apply to a lot of things in life. Some of the wants she couldn't have just hurt worse than others.

Kayla took Sophia by the arm and led her out of the barn.

"That's some kind of male testosterone back there in the barn. Hot damn." Sophia fanned her face.

"Don't let Ethan hear you say that." Kayla laughed.

"How is it between you and Dylan? Are you two okay? I was worried you'd be upset with me, but, all things considered, it was the way everything fell into place," Sophia said.

"It's okay. All things considered." Sophia's words said it all. "It was a long time ago."

"But you still have feelings, don't you? I saw the way you were watching him."

"Hardly. I've moved on, and we know I never mattered to him." Kayla didn't want to go down this road.

"What if you're wrong?" Sophia stopped and looked her dead in the eye.

"What do you mean?" she asked, the words tumbling out before she could stop them.

"What if he's still interested in you?"

She remembered the hungry look in his eyes. It didn't mean a thing. She'd seen the look once before. "He's not. And besides, I'm not interested." Turning up the compost of their past would serve no purpose.

Sophia would be yet another person to add to the list of those disappointed when she made the announcement about her new partnership with the veterinary clinic. Everyone expected her to move home, and there had been many times she'd considered doing that, but all along, she'd known in her heart she could never be this close to Dylan and be happy. No one knew the reality of what kept her away, and telling anyone now wouldn't change a thing.

Back at the house, Kayla headed for the kitchen in search of her mother and Derek. "How you making out, Derek?" she asked, surprised to see him helping her mother pull a casserole out of the oven.

"I'm helping your mom cook." He grinned. "I'm feeling better, and she really needed me. Everyone else is too busy to help her."

Derek was a great kid who obviously wanted to feel needed and to feel important. Just like every other kid. There was nothing wrong with him a little love and attention wouldn't correct.

"That's sweet of you. Thanks. Glad you feel better." Kayla winked.

"You're growing like a weed, but as handsome as ever, Derek. It's nice to see you again," Sophia said, ruffling the boy's hair.

"Um, thanks I guess. Good to see you, too." Derek's face turned red. He was a good-looking kid, just like his brother, but he was clearly not used to compliments.

"Sophia and I are going to sit on the porch swing and chat. You have everything under control here with your assistant?" she asked her mom.

"Everything is right on schedule. Dinner at seven, and then I think everyone's going to hang out for a while, but not too late. Big day tomorrow. You'll make a beautiful bride, Sophia."

"Thanks for letting me have the wedding here, Aunt Mary. I wish my mom and dad were here," Sophia said, a faraway look on her face.

Her mother reached out to pat her cousin's arm. "Honey, they are. They are always in our hearts. No one can take that away from you."

"Thank you," Sophia said, dropping a kiss on her mother's cheek.

No truer words could ever be said. Once a person was in your heart, it was impossible to get rid of them. Dylan was proof. In their case, hate was a fine line from love. Both were strong, powerful emotions people had little control over.

"Run along, you two, and have a nice chat. Once those guys get here, you won't get a word in edgewise." Her mother shooed them toward the door.

"Don't we know it," they both said in unison, laughing.

"Oh, by the way, Kayla, I didn't think of it yesterday, but the bride and groom can't sleep together the night before their wedding. We'll need to put Ethan in the spare room and Sophia in with you."

"Sure thing. I'll get the room ready."

"I don't want to cause any extra work," Sophia chimed in.

"It's not a problem," her mother said.

They had barely sat down when the group of men came around to the front of the house. The wedding cavalry must have finished their work.

"Hey, guys. Everything done?" Kayla and Sophia stood as

the men piled onto the front porch, grabbing chairs wherever they could find one.

"Done as done gets," Randy said.

Ethan promptly sat down on one of the vacant seats, and planted Sophia on his lap. "Hey, baby, miss me?" Ethan asked, grinning as he nuzzled the side of Sophia's cheek.

"Get a room, you two. Oh, that's right, you can't," Randy teased. "Wedding night no-no."

"What do you mean?" Ethan frowned.

"It means you get to sleep alone tonight." Dylan laughed.

"Where the hell am I supposed to sleep then?" Ethan's grin disappeared like the setting sun. Slow but sure.

"Mary's putting Sophia in with Kayla, and you get the spare guest room. She almost forgot the old tradition until I reminded her this afternoon," Dylan said and grinned. "You don't want to start your marriage off with bad luck in the bedroom."

"Laugh all you want, dude, because after tomorrow, I'll be sleeping with my bride for the rest of my life. Small price to pay for good luck in the bedroom, not that we need luck. Everything's fine in that department."

"Ethan!" Sophia gasped.

Ethan's chuckle turned into hearty laughter at Sophia's shocked expression. The rest of the guys joined in at Sophia's expense. Poor girl. Marrying a cowboy was never easy, but damn if it didn't have some good perks.

"Awww. So sweet and yuck. Boring," Randy joked.

"Your day will come, and then you'll be singing a different tune, cowboy," Kayla spoke up. "Some cute little spitfire is going to wrap you up tight and put a ring on that finger before you can say giddy up."

"You applying, sugar?" Randy asked her, a wide grin splitting his face.

"No, not likely," Kayla said.

"Every one of you will meet your special someone someday," her father chimed in.

"Dinner," her mother called from in the house. Everyone filed inside, one by one taking a seat at the giant picnic-style table used for old-fashioned family dinners. Home cooking at its finest, and her mom had gone all out for the occasion.

How in the heck she ended up with Dylan next to her was beyond her, but it wouldn't surprise her if the guys didn't have it planned that way. Up to no good.

Dylan leaned in close. "Can you pass me the potatoes, please?"

His breath tickled her cheek. A simple question, about potatoes no less, but her heart raced a little faster.

"Everything goes all the way around. You'll have to wait your turn."

"I know that. Checking to see if you remember how country folk eat a family dinner. None of the city's highfalutin ways rubbed off on you yet, have they?" Dylan's voice sent a warm heat down her spine.

"Who's watching the bar while you're here playing groom?" Randy asked Ethan.

"Someone dependable, no worries. I've been giving Becky more and more responsibility, so I can relinquish control enough to take my bride on a honeymoon. Tomorrow, I'm closing the place down so all my employees can attend."

Becky? It was a small town, but surely he didn't mean Becky McAllister.

"Wow. He must really love you, darling. I don't think the place has ever been closed since his daddy opened it up twenty years ago." Randy spoke to Sophia, but everyone nodded in agreement.

"That's good to hear considering half the fire department will be here dancing and drinking. One less place open is one less place to have a problem and pull me away," Tommy added.

"I've given the ranch hands the day off after the morning rounds," Dylan said. "I wouldn't want to stand in the way of anyone sharing in your joy of holy bondage," he teased.

Dylan's leg bumped hers. It wasn't the first time through the meal. Accidental or not, she wasn't certain, but each time, a sizzle of electricity rocketed through her body.

Grateful when the meal ended, Kayla needed to put distance between her and Dylan. Pushing back her chair, she rose. "Go on outside, all of you. I'll take care of the dishes since Mom cooked," she announced. Cleaning was the lesser of two evils if it came to that or going onto the front porch to join the others, or more specifically, Dylan."

It didn't take long for the room to clear out, everyone murmuring their thanks and praise for the great meal as they left. You didn't have to tell a cowboy twice to get out if it meant not having to do kitchen work.

Kayla stacked the plates and carried them to the kitchen, enjoying the silence for the first time that evening.

Dishes clattered in the dining room. She pushed the door open to see who had come back to help.

Dylan.

"Thought I'd give you a hand," he said.

"Why?" *So much for a peaceful few minutes.*

"Because there are a lot of dishes."

"No. Why you? Shouldn't you be out with the guys?" It was safer for her if he was out on the porch. Being alone with him would stir up memories best left forgotten.

"I've been waiting for a chance to talk to you. We were friends for a long time before we had sex. We have to talk about it some time."

Her eyes widened at his blunt words. This was so not a conversation she intended to have here in her mother's dining room with a group of people not thirty feet away.

"Shhhh." She cast a nervous glance back at the door.

"And, no, we don't. There's nothing to talk about."

"Kayla, please. Give me a break. It's been five years." He took a step closer and reached out to stop her from walking away. "Talk to me."

She pulled away and went back into the kitchen. She rinsed the dishes without a word, hoping he'd get the message and leave.

Instead, he proceeded to load the dishwasher quietly. Side by side.

He was asking her for something she couldn't give. Talking about the past would open old wounds, some of which he knew nothing about and were best left in the dark.

Nearly finished, Dylan came up behind her and placed one hand on each side of her head against the cupboard doors, trapping her in place without a touch.

"Listen to me. I'm sorry for walking away and hurting you. But it was the only way, you have to believe me."

She turned to face him, all pretense of calm evaporating.

"No, it wasn't the only way. It was your way. And you lost more than me that day, and you can't get any of it back. Please leave me alone. The past can't be undone."

"You're right, it was my way. But it was necessary. I can't undo walking away, but damn, are you going to crucify me for doing what was best for you?"

"Doing what was best for me? You're not serious? You did what was best for you."

"If that's what you believe, you don't know me very well. I couldn't let you stay. I couldn't let you wither away and die like my mother." His voice ached with pain as he poured out the last words.

What was he saying? His mother died in a car crash. What did any of this have to do with her? She couldn't stand here and listen to him. It was too late. Everything was too late. "Go away, Dylan."

Chapter Seven

It took Dylan great restraint not to say more and instead, make his way out to join the others. There were other ways to get his message across to her.

The squeak of the screen door announced his arrival, and all eyes turned in his direction.

"Everything all right?" Kayla's mother asked. Her frown was more telling than the actual words. Dylan needed to set Mary and Lou straight and stop their interfering ways.

"Right as rain." Something in short supply around here.

"You playing tonight?" Ethan asked from the corner of the porch where he sat with Sophia snuggled on his lap.

Dylan always played at their get-togethers, and he wasn't about to let the scene in the kitchen change anything. "Yep. Guitar's in the truck. I'll be right back."

He stepped off the porch and made his way to the truck, the sound of voices and laughter filling the night air behind him. He opened the case and withdrew his guitar, grabbing an extra pick, just in case. Tonight, he would honor the love between Sophia and Ethan. A love that was written in the stars and tangible.

The kind he'd shared with Kayla for a fleeting moment of time.

Dylan stepped back up on the porch, an idea taking hold. When the time was right, he'd slip in an extra song for Kayla.

And he knew just the song.

He settled in on the bench in the corner by the door and faced the group. Picking a few strings, he tuned the guitar, playing a few chords to loosen up his fingers. The group quieted in anticipation of the first song, eager to sing along with the campfire favorites he normally played. Lighthearted and popular, "Chicken Fried" was always one of the group's favorites, no party complete without it.

Kayla hadn't come out yet, and he wondered what was keeping her.

Dylan played two more songs before he broke into another ever-popular hit, "Sweet Caroline." The group sang and swayed together amidst tons of laughter and lots of beer. Randy and Tommy were as always, the life of the party with their little ad lib renditions along the way.

"Do 'Brown Eyed Girl,'" Ethan hollered. "In honor of the special brown-eyed girl marrying me tomorrow."

"Awww, I love you, too, honey." Sophia wrapped her arms around Ethan's neck and pulled his head down for a kiss.

"Save it for tomorrow night, you two," Tommy said, pushing them apart, to everyone's satisfaction and laughter.

• • •

Kayla listened to the group singing loudly and carrying on without a thought in the world except to have fun. It had been a long time since she'd experienced good old-fashioned country fun. Karaoke in a bar with hundreds of people, most of whom you didn't know, wasn't the same.

All heads turned to look when she pushed the squeaky door open and stepped out onto the porch. "Dishes are done. Hope you saved a few songs for me."

"Darling, where you're concerned, we would always have more songs," Randy teased. "But you're just in time for 'Brown Eyed Girl.' Come sit down over here by me. Plenty of room for your pretty self."

Kayla sat down in the chair Randy pulled up for her.

"By special request, this song is for a special lady tonight." Dylan let his fingers strum lightly over the strings before launching into the song.

His deep, sexy voice rumbled across the porch and down her spine and then back up, landing somewhere in the vicinity of her heart. He loved to sing as much as she loved to hear his voice. It seemed like only yesterday when she used to follow him around with her schoolgirl crush, hanging on to every word he sang as if he were singing to her and her alone. Back when she'd foolishly believed in happily ever after.

Kayla watched the happy couple dancing together, arm in arm—the world their own in that one special moment. By the second chorus, the group joined in, and Kayla found herself singing along.

The crowd was loud, but not loud enough to drown out someone singing the wrong words. She knew the voice too well not to recognize who changed the lyrics. Blue eyes. He'd sung it wrong on purpose.

Kayla turned to look back at Dylan and found him staring directly at her. She couldn't do this now. She had to shut him out. She turned back to watch the happy couple as Ethan dipped Sophia low and joined in the laughter.

It was hard not to feast her eyes on him, knowing he was singing the song to her. So far, no one else had noticed, but every word he sang made it harder and harder to ignore him.

Harder and harder to fight the memories of the way it used to be between them.

She managed to block out a few lines. Until he slipped the words "tree house" in there. Kayla cringed. *How dare he?*

There was no mistaking he was singing to her, taunting her with her greatest mistake. Well, she wasn't about to run. The first time, she'd fled to San Antonio and never looked back, but this time, she wasn't running. He could sing to the coyotes all night long, it meant nothing to her.

Moments ago, she was happy to join the group, almost like old times. Now she wanted nothing more than for the evening to end.

Loud clapping interrupted her wayward thoughts. She let out the breath she'd been holding. Thank goodness, the song was over.

"For this next one, I hope you will all indulge me a bit here. Ian Tyson's song isn't one of the normal ones I play, but one I'd like to do in honor of Kayla coming home."

No. No. No. No more. He wasn't playing fair. Kayla sat there speechless, unsure of what to say without sounding ungrateful.

Several people uttered their approval, and Dylan strummed a few chords, easing into the music softly.

The group was silent.

Kayla closed her eyes to fight the tears. Dylan knew exactly what he was doing. The song choice and words told a tale of lost love. It wasn't fair. He was the one who'd walked away. He was the one who'd left her alone to deal with the bitter pain of rejection. He was the one who'd thrown away every drop of her love with his betrayal.

He'd kicked her out of his life without a second thought. Never once had he tried to contact her.

But she'd survived, and she had a life.

It was asking too much to force her to sit here and listen,

but she had no choice. How many others sitting here knew the truth of why he'd chosen this song? Did they all know, or was this her own private misery? She didn't have the courage to look around at the group who had fallen completely and utterly silent while Dylan sang the heartfelt tune that reached deep into her soul.

The music stopped. Her heart stopped. Kayla opened her eyes and looked at Dylan. Big mistake. No one else existed for the space of what felt like eternity. In reality, it was only seconds.

But it was too late. Nothing could erase the memory of the twist the winding river took all those years ago.

· · ·

Dylan knew from the tears he'd seen pooling in Kayla's eyes, she had understood the song perfectly, but what she chose to do about it was out of his control for the time being. Just like another sleepless night had been out of his control.

"Morning," Dylan said as Derek entered the kitchen. He could have sworn it was Saturday, but his brother was never up this early on weekends.

"Good morning." Derek smiled.

Dylan wasn't sure what to make of his brother's behavior as he poured a glass of orange juice and sat down to eat his breakfast as if this were his normal routine. And there was no evidence of the boy who'd claimed to be sick enough to miss school yesterday.

Derek's chipper attitude had Dylan puzzled. "What's got you up before the birds?"

"Going for a ride with Kayla, um, if that's okay with you?" he asked, his voice hopeful.

Dylan did a double take. Asking permission wasn't normally part of the program lately. The brothers both had

Kayla on the brain, but it would seem Derek was the only one making progress.

Out of bed early, mindful of his manners, and suddenly remembering the rules. It was as if Derek had become a different kid overnight. Leave it to a woman to make the impossible possible. And not just any woman. Kayla.

It irritated him to no end.

Dylan had tried everything to reach the kid, and sweet-talking Kayla had waltzed in and succeeded where he was failing. She'd lied to cover Derek skipping school, something he downright disapproved of, but whatever else she was doing was working wonders.

He didn't have it in him to wipe away the first sign of happiness he'd seen in his brother in a while, but later, maybe after the wedding, they'd have their talk about skipping school. He couldn't let it slide.

"Just the two of you?" Dylan asked with undisguised interest.

"Yeah. She wanted to go out early and I don't think she should be riding alone." It appeared the kid had learned something. Chivalry wasn't dead.

"I have to agree with you. Thanks for stepping up and looking after her."

Derek shot him a funny look.

He wasn't averse to handing out praise, so it shouldn't be such a shock, but lately, there hadn't been many praise-worthy actions from his brother to compliment. Contrary to Kayla's opinion, he wasn't a heartless jerk.

"Do you like her? I heard you all talking, and it made me wonder." Derek stopped eating his bowl of cereal to look up as he waited for an answer.

A little truth wouldn't hurt either one of them. "I do. When she was about your age, she used to tag along and follow me everywhere like a little sister."

"So why isn't she like a sister now? And why doesn't she live here anymore?" His questions held the raw simplicity of youth.

"Because the brother-sister relationship got lost along the way, and something more powerful took its place. But Kayla was restless in the quiet of the country, and her dreams took her far away from Riverbend."

"Sounds like me. But why would you let her go? I like her, and I want her to stay."

"I let her go because of the more powerful thing I mentioned. Someday you'll understand. For me, her happiness was important, and she wasn't happy here, so I let her go."

"Doesn't she like you anymore? Maybe we could make her happy and want to stay," Derek offered in his innocence.

"No. Unfortunately, we can't. Only she can make herself happy, but it doesn't mean her friends can't give her an extra push to stop long enough and take a good look around. To see if it's a place she could love now that she's older and wiser." He winked.

"Is that what you're doing? Like that sappy song you did last night."

"Yeah, but how about keeping that between me and you? Our little secret."

Derek's grin warmed him. They were on the same side for a change. For both their sakes, he hoped Kayla stuck around.

"Sounds like a plan. So, um, if you *like* like her, why don't you come with us this morning? You never ride with me for fun. It's always work, work, work. Maybe if you showed her you could be fun, she'd like you better."

The kid was right. There was always work to be done. The ranch and all the people he employed depended on him. And it was his job to make sure Derek had everything he needed.

He was only one person, but it didn't stop the guilt as he

tried to figure out the easiest way to say no. Maybe, just this once, he could say yes. It wasn't like the ranch hands wouldn't take care of what needed to be done, but for him, shrugging responsibility didn't come easy.

There'll always be something else unless I make a change. Riding out with Derek and Kayla sounded like as good a time as any to play hooky. Not to mention Derek made a good point, if he joined them on the ride, it would give him another opportunity to press forward with his plan to show Kayla what she was missing. Using his brother to get closer to Kayla had never occurred to him, but it certainly would make things easier. Kayla wouldn't back out on Derek.

Maybe he wouldn't be having that talk with his brother at all. "Okay."

"Really? You mean it? Thanks." His brother's eyes lit up like it was Christmas morning and Santa had delivered his number-one request. Something as simple as a ride. Something his father had never done with Dylan. It was always work, work, work.

And in the end, Dylan had rebelled to get his attention. The Fearless Five all had their reasons for stirring up trouble, but all Dylan had ever managed to get was a switch and more chores. No time. No praise. No love.

Exactly like his mother had never felt loved. Steeped in tradition, had he ignored the truth and carried on like his father instead of making a change? His father had died working, and Dylan couldn't remember a time when he'd seen him happy. Did he want to be like his father? A man who drove his wife away from the ranch that imprisoned her?

Like he'd driven Kayla away five years ago, terrified to watch her wilt away as the ranch sucked the beauty and joy from her life. In the end, wasn't it the same thing? They'd both driven away the woman they loved. For the first time, Dylan saw his life differently, and he didn't like what he saw.

He'd become his father.

. . .

Two riders approached on horseback, their figures dark against the backdrop of the breaking dawn. One tall and proud, confident in the way he rode, the other shorter and not quite as smooth. Dylan and Derek.

Yesterday, Dylan had made it clear his brother wasn't her concern, but Kayla couldn't believe he would go so far as to join them on the early morning ride because of his lack of trust in her abilities. Grateful he hadn't taken the ride away from the kid, she would tolerate his presence. Barely.

The pleasure on Derek's face last night had been genuine when she'd invited him to ride out this morning. It felt right to try and bring even a smidgeon of happiness to the boy's life, even if she had to endure Dylan riding shotgun.

Derek hadn't liked her condition that he ask Dylan for permission, but she'd held her ground. And the price of her insistence came in the form of the man himself. As much as she didn't want Dylan around, his presence would be like whipped cream on an apple dumpling treat to his little brother.

"Morning, Kayla," Derek called out excitedly before they reached the barn where she waited. "Hope you don't mind, but I invited my brother." A wide, crooked-tooth grin on his face won her over.

"Of course not. Good morning to you both." She couldn't keep her gaze from traveling to Dylan.

"Good morning, Kayla. It's going to be another hot day."

Weather was always a safe topic. "And dry from what I hear," she added.

"I'm sure Sophia won't mind the dryness this afternoon," he said. "Although maybe if it rains it'll be considered a good luck omen for their marriage, considering the drought."

"I'll have to agree with you there."

"Music to my ears." He steadied his horse as he pawed at the ground, anxious to be off on the morning ride.

Another cryptic comment. One she wasn't about to let slide. "What do you mean?"

"You agreeing with me on something. Maybe we could make it a habit."

She'd fallen right into the trap, and damn if he hadn't delivered the smooth-talking line like it was rehearsed. But it didn't mean she had to take a bite of the apple he offered.

"Speaking of weddings, we need to ride. We don't have much time before we have to get back."

Derek looked back and forth between them, his brow creased in a tight frown. "I think it's cool you're both in the wedding. Maid of honor and best man."

"I couldn't agree with you more." Dylan cast a sly smile her way before he spurred his horse forward, cutting off any chance of a reply.

They fell into an easy canter, side by side, with Kayla in the middle. Heading east, the rising sun crested the horizon in full streaks of red, painting the edges of nearby clouds.

"Wow, it's breathtakingly gorgeous out here this time of the morning," she said.

"I have to agree." Dylan wasn't looking at the sunrise.

Kayla chose to ignore the comment, but it didn't stop her heart from pounding. *Traitorous organ.*

A compliment from Dylan was like the first few drops of rain in a storm. Exciting. But if they continued, they could lead to a flood of emotions she wasn't prepared to handle. She'd been a fool to think she could come here and not have old feelings rise and bite her in the derriere, and if last night's performance was any indicator, she was in trouble. For whatever reason, she was back on Dylan's radar.

Many women admitted they never got over their first love, but most moved on to live happy lives.

"Look, Kayla," Derek exclaimed. His hand shot forward and pointed to a place where three deer grazed in the distance.

"They're beautiful. Good eye." The kid beamed under her praise.

For the next hour, they talked and rode. A sense of peace settled over her like a well-worn pair of faded jeans. Soft and snug, almost caressing. This was her home. Her land.

Well, her parents' land, anyway. Someday it would be hers, but the million-dollar question remained. What would she do with it? Rich with family history, generations of Andersons had been born and raised here, creating the very essence of the land. Home.

And other than the man riding next to her, home felt good.

A little action would help keep her mind off the guilt she felt for leaving in the first place, and now, for the regret simmering at the surface. It wouldn't do any good for regret to worm its way into her heart. She'd made her choice, and there was no turning back.

"Race you guys to the grove of trees over there," she said, pointing to a spot in the distance off to the left.

"What's the bet?" Derek asked in excitement.

"Sign of true cowboy. Gotta have a bet," Dylan added with a grin, his words earning him an award-winning smile from Derek.

"Losers take care of the winner's horse when we get back?" Kayla offered.

"That'll work. But it's probably not fair, because Kayla hasn't ridden in a while. Maybe we shouldn't bet," Dylan said. His lips twitched, trying to keep a straight face. She knew what he was doing, but damned if she could shut her mouth.

"I can ride. Just because I haven't ridden in a while doesn't mean I don't know what I'm doing. Challenge accepted."

Dylan was sure to win anyway, and Kayla figured it was a safe bet. One that would leave her and Derek brushing down Dylan's horse.

"Fine. You call the start," Dylan said, nodding toward her.

"Yes!" Derek's excitement was contagious as Kayla readied herself to take flight with Dizzy. The mare was getting older, but Kayla was determined to make the race look good for the boy's sake.

"Three. Two. One. Go." They all took off like a shot, Kayla getting a head start as she rattled off the words, lickety-split quick, catching them off-guard.

Exhilaration filled her. On and on, the horse's hooves pounded the ground in a fast rhythm. Her hair whipped around her face. Kayla peeked back to check her lead, dismayed to see them both close on her heels. So much for a lead.

"Come on, Dizzy girl," she said, leaning forward and becoming one with her mare, working together. Just like old times.

Seconds passed. Dylan's massive horse pulled up close and then surged ahead after he tossed her a brief challenging cat-got-the-cream grin. Kayla looked around for Derek, surprised to see him pull neck and neck with her. Miniature Dylan was going to give her a run for the money, although Kayla had every intention of letting him beat her anyway. Every kid needed a confidence booster now and then, and today was Derek's lucky day.

As they neared the trees, Dylan was in the lead, positioned to win. Kayla slowed slightly to let Derek move ahead. At the last second, Dylan pulled up on his reins no more than fifty feet from the finish line, and Derek shot forward to claim the win. It all happened so fast, Kayla was still in shock as she reined in her mare.

Her worry for Dylan's horse superseded the price of losing the bet. She raced to his side. "Is he okay? Did he come up lame?" Kayla jumped off her horse and ran her hands down the gelding's legs.

"Relax. He's fine. He stumbled, and I pulled up to be safe." Dylan stood next to the massive Quarter Horse, but he didn't seem nearly as concerned as he should be.

Which could only mean one thing. "Did you just throw the race?" She stood and looked him straight in the eye.

"Hardly. Why would I?" he said, a look of pure innocence. Cat-got-the-cream innocent. She didn't trust him, but her answer was cut short when Derek pulled up next to them.

"Congratulations, Derek," Kayla said.

"Great run. You've gotten pretty good since I last rode with you," Dylan said.

"It has been a while, but thanks." Derek beamed, his cheeks flushed with pleasure. High praise from Dylan meant the world to the kid.

"How about I see what I can do to change some things around, so we can do it more often?"

"Really? You mean it? That would be awesome. Winning is pretty awesome, too, because you two get to brush down my horse when we get back, and for once, I can get out of a chore without getting in trouble." He laughed.

"How about that? Miracles do happen." Dylan's laughter matched his brother's.

The rat. He'd done it on purpose. How ironic. She'd let Derek beat her for a confidence booster only to find out Dylan was thinking the same thing, but she was certain his reasons weren't nearly as altruistic as hers.

Chapter Eight

"See you later," Derek said, handing the reins to Dylan and taking off for the house like a jackrabbit. The kid was quite pleased with himself, if his grin was anything to go by.

Dylan came to stand next to her, his nearness sending shivers down her spine even though it was eighty-five degrees outside.

"How do you want to do this? Each do our own and then brush down Jezebel together?" he asked.

"I guess. I'm still thinking you lost on purpose, and I haven't forgiven you yet, so I might let you do Jezebel all by yourself." She would never back out on her part of the bargain, but there was no harm in taunting him.

"I plead the Fifth, but I can't believe you would welch on a bet just to avoid me. I don't bite."

"That remains to be seen."

Kayla was in over her head and had no idea how to swim in the sea of emotions threatening to drown her. It was easier to stay focused on Dizzy, each pull of the brush delivered with precise, long strokes. Anything to keep her mind off

Dylan standing less than ten feet away.

She stalled as long as possible, to the point Dizzy nudged her shoulder as if to urge her on. The mare wanted her reward and was impatient. Kayla took the lead and led Dizzy back to her stall where fresh hay and an apple would be expected.

Dylan had already started on Jezebel, but it was only fair since she thought he threw the race. They hadn't said more than ten words while they groomed their horses, leaving Kayla to wonder what he was thinking. It wouldn't be as easy to ignore him when they worked side by side, but for her peace of mind, she would try.

"'Bout time you got to your end of the deal. Figured you were moving at a snail's pace to make sure I did all the work," Dylan said. His eye-crinkling, sexy smile melted her resistance to fight back.

"I was, but since I consider myself an honorable person, I couldn't not help. No matter how much it pains me to work with you." She had to remember the reality between them. She had to stay strong against the charm he wore like a second skin.

"Kayla. Stop. It doesn't have to be this way between us." He stopped brushing, one hand on the mare's head to hold her still. His gaze seared Kayla with its intensity, but she kept stroking Jezebel. She wasn't about to let him see how much he was affecting her.

"Yes, it does. I'm glad you walked away, but it didn't make it hurt any less at the time." There. She'd said it. Maybe saying it would finally put an end to the mind-numbing hold strangling her emotions.

"I'm sorry. I would have given anything not to hurt you. Sleeping with you was a mistake, and it made it ten times harder to let you go."

"A mistake," she said, her voice tight. "That's what you're calling it?"

Her pile-of-crap meter overflowed.

"You don't know the flipping meaning of a mistake," she continued before he had a chance to answer. "Just like you have no idea how much your mistake cost me. Us. You walked away and never looked back. It took me years to get over your betrayal and the pain of rejection, and all I ask for now is for you to leave me alone. I can't go through it again." Her voice was a strangled whisper and foreign to her ears.

So much for not showing how much he affected her.

"That's twice you've alluded to something in the past, and I don't have a clue what you're talking about. What happened, Kayla?" He took a step closer.

She'd said too much already, and she'd be damned if she'd spill her guts now. It was over.

"Nothing. It's in the past where it belongs."

"Any chance you're not over me? Because I'm a long way from being over you, darling."

"Sorry, can't fix the damage you did. Not now. Not ever. Don't do this to me, please." She stepped away, needing the distance like a shield of armor against his words. Tears welled up, and she fought to hold them off. The last thing she wanted to do was cry in front of him. Over him. Not anymore. That part of her life was history.

"Why not now?" He scowled.

"There's too much bad history. I'm…" *No.* She wouldn't do it. Wouldn't tell him about the past. It would serve no purpose to dredge up painful memories.

"You're what?" he persisted.

The lump in her throat made it hard to swallow. "I'm leaving in a few days. My life is in the city, and I've worked hard to get where I'm at. No way I'm letting anything get in the way, and most certainly not anyone. Especially you. You had your chance, and you threw me away like a rotted sack of horse feed."

The words came out all wrong. She sounded more like a wounded girl crying out for attention than someone over and done with the past.

Mistake. Yeah, it was a mistake all right, her biggest one.

"But what if you're wrong? What if you're not really a city girl and your heart is here?" Dylan's words echoed in her head over and over. Her heart. Her heart would always be here, but her reality was not her heart. She wouldn't be deceived twice.

"It's not," she said with finality. "I've got to go." Kayla turned and ran for the house just in time. Tears slid down her face unchecked, but at least Dylan hadn't seen them.

"Kayla, wait," he called out after her. Nothing would get her to turn around and go back. Dylan was right where he needed to be. In her past.

Kayla reached the house and brushed away her tears. She had to pull herself together and help Sophia get ready for the wedding, get herself ready, and be down at the barn by one. Tall order and not much time.

She grabbed her emerald-green gown from the closet along with all her accessories and headed for the door, ready to take on her bridesmaid duties. The staging area had been set up in the extra bedroom, and she was already late.

"Knock knock. Everyone decent? I'm coming in," she called out, one hand on the knob. The door was flung open and Kayla was grabbed by the arm and yanked inside.

"Where have you been? We've been looking all over for you. Sophia's in the bathroom crying because her hair isn't right, and she woke up with a big red spot on her chin." Jennie was a good friend of Sophia's, and if her frazzled condition was any indicator, there was big trouble.

"Calm down. You two finish getting ready, and I'll talk to Sophia." The two women looked grateful she'd arrived. Kayla dropped her things on the bed before knocking on the bathroom door.

"Sophia, it's me. Let me in."

The door opened immediately, and Kayla was shocked to find Sophia exactly as Jennie had described. She'd expected some exaggeration, but there was none. Sophia's hair was a disaster. and the spot Jennie mentioned was in fact a woman's wedding day nightmare.

"Look at me, I'm a mess," Sophia said, her eyes red and puffy from crying. "Ethan's going to run the other way when he gets one good look at me today."

"Shhhh. It'll be okay. We can take care of this, but I need you to stop crying, because red puffy eyes will last for hours if you don't."

"You really think you can fix me?" Sophia asked, hope lacing her words as she wiped the tears away.

"Yes. The spot on your face is from stress and your hair is probably from the hard water we have here at the farm. Both things I've dealt with."

She poked her head out the door. "Can one of you get me some ice, a tube of toothpaste, and the jar of honey?"

They all looked at her like she'd lost her mind, but Sophia had stopped crying, and that's all that mattered.

"Right away. Thanks, Kayla. You're a life saver," Megan said.

Two hours later, Sophia looked every inch the beautiful bride. Her hair curled around her face in silky waves. Her skin appeared flawless with the help of a little extra makeup. And her dress was the crowning glory.

A masterpiece of delicate white lace, it hung down low in the back but barely passed her knees in the front, revealing Sophia's long legs and cowboy boots. The boots she'd chosen matched her raven-black hair, the combination stunning.

Jennie and Megan couldn't believe their eyes. "What did you do with that stuff? It's a miracle."

Kayla laughed. "Good old home remedies I learned living on the farm. What do you say we go get you hitched?" she asked Sophia.

"Thanks. You're the best." Sophia took one last look in the mirror and grinned from ear to ear. "Yee haw," she hollered. "I'm gonna go rope me a cowboy."

. . .

Kayla was about to walk down the aisle with Dylan toward a preacher. Not exactly the way she'd planned it all those years ago, considering it wasn't their wedding.

For months, she'd tortured herself with the images of Becky and Dylan getting married after her mother told her Becky was pregnant, but it had never happened. Kayla knew the truth about their son, even if they hadn't admitted it to the world, and she would have given anything to switch places with Becky, married or otherwise.

Some of the time, she went so far as to torture herself and imagine the way it could have been if his love had been real. She pictured Dylan coming home every night after a long day, to her and their son. She would have been the perfect rancher's wife. Her love had been strong enough for them both. *But would it have been enough?*

Kayla stepped back to take in the finished wedding decorations. Silver and gold stars hung from the rafters, the effect dazzling with the miniature lights draped across the ceiling. Red-checkered tablecloths covered the tables set up around the wedding aisle and dance floor. Dozens of locals had shown up to witness the pair tie the knot, and beyond the tables, more people stood gathered around to watch the wedding.

It may be a small community, but it was filled with down-home goodness and love.

Kayla moved to stand next to Dylan at the entrance to

the barn. Dressed in a long black tuxedo jacket, black jeans, and black cowboy boots, he looked every bit like a rogue lawman, especially with his black cowboy hat tipped down low. A silver bolo tie and huge silver belt buckle finished the image off perfectly. He could have stepped right off the set of *Gone with the Wind*.

She glanced down at her emerald-green dress. Satin and lace and every bit designed like something a Southern belle would wear. Had Sophia planned this all along? Rhett Butler and Scarlett O'Hara.

Kayla shook her head, disgusted by the image of them together. Did Sophia perhaps forget that Rhett rode off and left Scarlett at the end of the movie? She'd already lived that scene once, and once was enough.

Dylan turned to face her when the postmistress moved away to chat up someone else.

"You look beautiful. More beautiful than ever." His deep, husky voice made her want to believe.

"Dylan…"

"Relax. How about a truce for the rest of the day? For Sophia and Ethan's sake," he said quietly.

It would be petty not to agree. The past was over, and today being her cousin's wedding day, it was the right thing to do.

"Okay. Just for today." Her heart dropped to the pit of her stomach when his sexy country-cowboy smile beamed down at her. She might have just made a deal with the devil.

"Thank you. You won't regret it," he said, reaching for her hand and placing it on his arm. "You ready?"

"As ready as I'll ever be."

The music started, and Kayla watched as the first two bridesmaids and groomsmen made their way down the path created through the middle of the barn. Too soon, it was their turn. Dylan's commanding presence and firm grip kept her from running away. It was too much like her dream, except she wasn't wearing white. One foot in front of the other, she kept walking. Smiling, happy faces turned to watch them come down the aisle. Together. Like a couple. Dylan squeezed her hand as if sensing her distress.

The crowd became a sea of faces, a blur. Except one. Kayla locked eyes with Becky. Everything else around her faded to black. It was the first time she'd laid eyes on her ex-best friend since the last time they spoke. Five years ago, Becky hadn't even had the good grace to lie when Kayla had accused her of seeing Dylan behind her back. Pain sliced through her heart as she remembered.

Betrayal. Becky. Baby.

She hadn't prepared for this moment, because wherever Becky went, there was sure to follow a little brown-haired boy who would probably look exactly like Dylan.

Kayla fought the rising tide of nausea threatening to consume her. Dylan's touch burned into her skin. She steeled herself for the punch as she scanned the guests nearby in search of the child. Nothing.

Maybe she'd get lucky and Becky would have found a babysitter for the occasion.

Dylan dropped her arm when they reached the end, leaving her to stand on her side of the aisle, and he on his. The loss of contact gave her a moment of relief from the feelings threatening to overwhelm her. Everyone was in place as they waited for the bride. Ethan beamed in anticipation. All eyes turned to the barn door, but Kayla watched Dylan instead. She already knew what the bride looked like so she used the moment to watch him.

Why does he look sad? There was a quiet resignation in the way he held himself as he watched Sophia and her dad walk down the aisle.

Kayla followed his gaze. Her dad had been honored to

stand up for Sophia, and he looked every inch the part of the doting father. He was still a handsome devil, and she could totally understand why her mother loved him. But had her mother always been happy or had she wanted more once upon a time?

It was a question she'd never thought to ask before.

She glanced back at Dylan, only to find his gaze locked on her. Words weren't necessary. Kayla saw longing and regret, and it broke her heart just a little bit more. It wasn't fair. He didn't have the right to make her hurt.

Kayla turned back to watch Sophia. She wiped at her tears furiously with the back of her hand. Thankfully, everyone would assume it was because of the wedding.

The simple ceremony was beautiful. Two people. One love. And every part of the ceremony echoed the love between the happy couple. All too soon, the tables and chairs were pushed back to make room for the dance floor, and the music started. Sophia looked radiant in Ethan's arms as they moved to the dance floor for their first dance as man and wife.

The song ended, and the guitar player stepped up to the mike. It should have been Dylan playing, but as one of the wedding party, he had other duties. Duties that would include spinning her around the dance floor. Her heart pounded loudly. She knew what was coming. Sophia had reminded her, but it's not like she could ever forget.

"And now if we could get the maid of honor, the best man, and the rest of the wedding party to join the bride and groom on the dance floor, we'll kick off this shindig."

Dylan crossed the room to her side. "May I have this dance?" He held out his arm.

"Yes." She laid her hand gently across his forearm.

Dylan led her to the far side of the dance floor. "I'm sorry about earlier." He pulled her tightly against his chest, one arm looped around her back, the other holding her hand out to lead her in a waltz.

"I don't want to discuss it," she said, trying to hold her body stiff against his.

"What do you want to talk about?"

"Let's not talk."

"Darling, we've done enough of that for five years. Don't you think it's time for a change? Besides, I don't think you're as immune to me as you claim to be."

Weddings were hell on a person's emotions, and being in Dylan's arms made it worse, but him calling her darling, well, that was over the top. His hand dropped to her waist, the contact burning through the thin layers of material that separated his hand from her skin.

"I don't know. Things are good the way they are. Why change it now?"

Kayla scanned the room as Dylan spun her around the dance floor. Anything other than looking up at Dylan and getting lost in the temptation his chocolate eyes offered.

"Are you happy in the city?" His question caught her off-guard.

"Wow. Where did that come from?" She tried to dodge the bullet.

"Answer the question. Are you happy?" he persisted.

How could she answer if she didn't know herself? Before she'd come to visit, the answer would have been easy. Time and being back home had changed her perspective about a lot of things. A lot of things except Dylan. He'd gotten older and possibly more charming, but nothing could change the past.

"Yes." It was the safest answer.

The city offered her the fun and excitement she'd originally longed for, but once the newness had worn off, she'd realized a lot of the people there were going through the motions of living, hopping from one party to the next, one event to the next, one dinner out to the next. There was always something going on, and people never stopped to get off the carousel and look around. To breathe.

She'd already considered moving home, but there was simply too much history in Riverbend, which was why she'd accepted the partnership offer.

"Have you ever thought of coming home?" he asked. It was like he could read her mind.

"Houston is my home now. I like it there."

He pulled her in closer. "And I like you here."

His words caused her to stumble. Here in Riverbend or here in his arms? Either way, his statement confused her.

She ignored his last words. "Why do you think Sophia and Ethan did this to us?" she asked bluntly. It wasn't a big secret she didn't want anything to do with Dylan.

"What makes you think it was planned?" he asked.

"They both know how things stand between us."

"Maybe they're trying to rewrite the ending." He pulled back to smile down at her.

"You think they're playing matchmaker? That's crazy."

"Is it?" He pulled her back in close, keeping her emotionally off-balance.

"Yes. It is. What things?"

"Maybe you should stick around a while. You might be surprised what you learn." He spoke the words like a lover imparting a secret.

She swallowed hard. "I can't. I'm leaving Wednesday. School starts back up soon, and clinic hours take up the rest of my time. They've offered me a partnership, and I've accepted. Life doesn't revolve around Riverbend for me anymore."

"Pity. It's not bad here. People have a way of making you feel wanted, there's a sense of community and pride. When times are tough, people help one another. There's a sense of belonging I never understood when I was younger."

It was hard to believe they were having a real conversation

for the first time in years.

"You don't regret giving up your dreams?" She hadn't planned on getting personal, but the question slipped out.

"Who said I gave them up?" he asked softly, his lips tickly close to her ear.

She pulled back to look at him in confusion. "You still want to ride in the rodeo?"

He laughed. "No, darling, my dream was much bigger. And a whole lot sweeter."

"Is that why you're expanding the herd beyond what you can sustain on your own ranch? It's a huge risk, and you could lose everything."

Dylan led her easily around the dance floor while they talked.

"It's definitely why I expanded. But you're wrong. I'm not beyond what I can sustain. The drought is making it hard on everyone, not just me, and we all do what we must to survive. Yes, I could lose everything, but I doubt it will get to that. I have things under control."

Dylan pulled her back in close and held tightly. His arm was a steel band around her waist. "Have you told your parents you're never coming back?"

"No. Not yet."

Just then, the song ended, and Dylan let her go. He looked deep into her eyes for a moment and then turned to leave. She watched him walk away before seeking out her parents. They wouldn't be happy hearing about the job offer in the city, but they did need to know.

As she made her way across the room, Kayla remembered the expression on Dylan's face. It was the same lost-puppy look she remembered when his mother died, and it tore at her heart.

When had things gotten so complicated? *When I came home, is when.* Specifically, when Dylan walked through the kitchen door.

"Hey, Mom, Dad." She sat down next to her parents. "There's something I wanted to tell you." She tried not to focus on the hopeful look in their eyes, so she could continue. "I've been offered a partnership at the clinic, and I'm going to take it."

"I don't understand." Her mother's shoulders tensed ever so slightly. "You don't need to make a decision like that until you've finished your last year. I always thought you'd come home."

She followed her mother's gaze to discover she was watching Dylan and Derek.

"Sweetheart, five years is a long time. Both you and Dylan are older now. Maybe it's time you were friends again and you both let the past go."

"It's not that easy. Please don't ask me to explain."

"You said *going* to accept. Does that mean you can still change your mind?" Leave it to her father to pick up on the little loophole of hope she'd used to soften the blow.

"Let's enjoy the time we have together. Okay?"

"Sure thing, honey." Her father hadn't said much, but it was what he didn't say that she found concerning. He'd accepted her declaration all too easily. He was up to something, she felt sure of it.

Kayla snuck a glance at Dylan again. Derek stood defensively in the corner, hands on his hips, an exact replica of Dylan as they squared off.

Watching from the sidelines, she didn't notice she had company until she felt a slight tug on her dress. A little boy around four years old looked up at her with dark-brown eyes and an angelic face. The same age her son would have been. Her heart clenched.

Unable to resist, she bent down to the child's level to talk to him. Watching other children play reminded her of what she'd lost, and she usually avoided interactions with kids. But everyone in Riverbend seemed to have a child, or two, or three, judging by the number of kids running around the barn.

"What's your name?' she asked.

"Bywan," he said, his grin producing a dimple on each side of his chubby little face. "Aww you my mommy's best friend?" he asked.

"Well, that depends on who your mommy is, now doesn't it, Byron?" She looked around and didn't see any mothers rushing up to corner the wandering boy and claim him.

"Mommy's name is Mommy, silly, Auntie Kaywa. I saw you in the pictures at my house."

She swallowed hard but couldn't speak. She wasn't anyone's Auntie Kaywa or Auntie Kayla for that matter. *Please don't let this be Becky's son.* Dylan's son. The brown eyes looking back at her could have been Dylan's. It wasn't fair. Kayla knew the truth but had to ask.

"Is your mommy…" she started to say, the words dying on her lips as Becky appeared to stand next to him.

"Yes, he's mine," Becky said, a tentative smile on her face.

Kayla felt faint. She couldn't do this. Her heart snapped in two. This was the moment she'd shied away from, and the biggest reason she stayed away from Riverbend. Meeting Dylan and Becky's son. It wasn't fair to the child Dylan had never claimed the boy, and it wasn't fair Kayla had lost her son. Byron was a beautiful reminder of a devastating past best left untouched. There was nothing she could say to make this moment right. To make this moment less painful. She turned and walked away, wiping her tears as she left.

From the corner of the room, she noticed when Becky left with Byron. Kayla wished she was the one leaving instead. In fact, she wished she'd never come to the wedding.

Chapter Nine

Never coming home. Dylan stared into his coffee cup, but it could have been gasoline for all he knew. Talk about a knockout punch when he wasn't looking. He was too late. Kayla had forgotten all about home and her roots. And him.

For years, his life had been guided by doing what was best for his brother, making the ranch successful, and hopefully, one day, winning back the girl he'd set free.

To all intents and purposes, his life was a failure. His brother couldn't wait to leave home, the ranch was barely making it, and he'd lost the girl. And to make matters worse, he wasn't the only Hunter male devastated by Kayla's news. Derek didn't want her to leave, either.

It had been hard to stay through the rest of the reception. It was obviously time to let go and move on with his life. And if it weren't for the little matter of the contract with her dad, he would. Neither of them had seen this coming when Lou sold him the farm. They both had mistakenly believed there was plenty of time before they had to declare their hand. They couldn't have been more wrong.

It had been risky to invest in the Anderson farm, since most of his capital was already tied up when he increased the herd. But he'd needed the land, or more specifically, he'd needed the river running through the land. Now, what the hell was he supposed to do? He was caught in a trap of his own making.

He should have never agreed to buy the farm or to the Kayla clause.

But Lou's plea for him to step in and buy the place to save it from bankruptcy had come at a time when Dylan had needed the water rights, and a deal had been struck that satisfied both men with regards to the future. A deal that revolved around Kayla, both men mistakenly under the assumption that one day she would return to Riverbend. To stay.

The Andersons had always been kind to him, and in Kayla's absence, he and his brother had become regular visitors at the farm. Mary and Lou were always more than happy to watch over his brother and lend a helping hand when times were rough. Their help was invaluable. The contract had been a way to pay them back for years of kindness.

He would have to talk to Lou about changing the contract, because after the bomb she dropped last night, the Kayla clause was no longer viable.

He took one sip of the cold coffee and spit it back in the cup. He crossed the kitchen to the sink and poured the contents down the drain. Sunday mornings were church time for most people in Riverbend, but Dylan's church was working out in the fields. Same thing he did every morning, and Kayla's announcement didn't change what needed to be done.

He filled his thermos and left a note for Derek. Kid would probably sleep until noon if he let him, and for once, Dylan was inclined to oblige. Today, he simply didn't have the energy or drive to fight with his brother about chores.

The phone attached to his hip vibrated, followed by a familiar ring tone.

"We got trouble," Leroy said after Dylan answered.

Dylan was instantly alert. If his herd manager said there was trouble, it was going to be a bad day.

"Shoot."

"One of the cows is in labor, and she's struggling. Been going on for over an hour and she's starting to look pretty wore out."

"Damn. Breech?"

"It would seem so. I can feel a tail and a tangle of legs. I'm not positive, but it could be twins."

"Is Jim on his way?" His vet would know exactly what to do, and even if Dylan couldn't afford the extra expense, he could afford to lose the cow and the calves even less.

"That's the bigger problem. He's out of town."

"Have you tried the vet over in Franklin to see if he'll come over?"

"Yup. He's tied up with a mare birthing twin foals. He estimated another couple of hours before he could get here, but he's put us next on the list."

"That's not good enough. They could all be dead by then. I'm on my way." Dylan ended the call and took off running in the direction of the barn.

"How's she doing?" Dylan asked as he moved to stand next to Leroy. He ran his hand down the girth of the cow.

"No change," Leroy said.

Dylan stripped off his shirt and sanitized his hands and arms before sliding a big plastic sleeve over his right arm. "Easy, girl. Let me see what's going on," he spoke in a soothing voice and slid his hand into the cow to see if he could help the calf get its legs in the right position.

If Leroy couldn't do it, chances were, he couldn't, either.

But it wouldn't stop him from trying.

"Hold her head. Don't let her try to push me away," Dylan ordered.

"Sure thing, boss." Leroy move to stand at the front of the stall.

"I see what you mean. The calf's legs seem tangled, but I can't reach in far enough to do any good. What about the gal in town at the regular vet clinic?" he asked in frustration.

"Tried her, too. She's over in Brighton on an emergency and can't get here any sooner than the other vet."

How could such a small area have three vets and not a damn one be available in an emergency? "There has to be someone we can call," he said. He ran his free hand through his hair.

"Not sure where things stand between you and Kayla, but I reckon you ought to call her."

Dylan tensed. As much as he hated to admit it, Leroy was right. Kayla might not want to help, but he had to ask. He'd do anything if there was a chance to save the cow and her calves.

He pulled off the sleeve and dialed the Anderson house.

"Good morning," Lou answered.

"Lou, it's Dylan."

"Hey there. About last night—"

"I don't have time to talk about it. I need Kayla," Dylan said, cutting right to the point.

"What do you mean?"

"I'm in the barn. Tell her I've got a breech calf, maybe twins."

"But she specializes in small animals, and she's got another year before she's licensed. Where's Jim?" he asked, a note of worry evident in his voice.

"He's out of town, and the others are out on other calls right now. She's the only person available within an hour's ride, and we've got to try something."

"Well, she did get her degree in Animal Science, and she's been working in a clinic for years. I reckon she may have learned something at that fancy city school of hers about farm animals."

"Thanks, Lou. See you in a few."

. . .

Kayla's heart pounded like a jackhammer, threatening to explode from her chest. Dylan had no idea what he was asking of her, or he wouldn't have bothered. She clutched her dad's arm tightly as they hurried into the barn, grateful for his presence and his reassurance.

"Kayla, over here," Dylan called.

"I don't know what I can do to help. You understand I specialized in small animals, and I'm not a vet yet, right?" she asked, vulnerability echoing in her voice.

"You have to try, please. You're the best we've got right now." Dylan was under a lot of strain, and she couldn't refuse to help him any more than she could refuse to help any animal in pain. But only as a last resort.

"There must be other vets available?"

"This ain't the city, darling. Vets here cover wide territories, and when they get called away, it can take a while to get someone out to the ranch. I'm sure you've learned something that will help. The cow is our primary concern at this point."

"Dylan, listen to me. I've studied farm animals, but I've only worked with small animals at the clinic. Nothing about a cow spells 'small animal'. You can't expect me to perform a miracle when I don't have the foggiest idea where to begin."

Reading about breeched calves in a textbook was not even remotely close to the real thing. If she failed, they would all blame her, but worse, if she didn't try and the animals died, they'd blame her anyway.

"I should have known you wouldn't help. I'm sorry I bothered you," he said, disappointment etched across his face. He turned back to his foreman. "How's she doing, Leroy?"

"Not good." Leroy looked at Kayla, a pleading look on his face.

Her father stepped in closer. "Kayla, no one will blame you if it doesn't work out, but give them a chance. This cow needs you."

They didn't understand everything that could go wrong. She knew the statistics, and they weren't good. Everyone was watching her, waiting for an answer. Kayla knew she didn't have a choice.

"Can someone get Doc on the phone to talk me through this? I can't promise anything, but I'll try."

Cheers erupted from the men standing nearby. The full impact of her commitment hit her square in the gut. They all believed in her and now she needed to believe in herself.

Dylan didn't say much, but then he'd already said enough. She was his last choice, just like before, and his faith in her had wavered before she'd even decided.

"Got Doc on the line," Leroy said, running over to her.

"Put him on speakerphone." He pressed a button and held out the phone.

"Doc, can you hear me? It's Kayla Anderson."

"Bless your heart for doing this. I ran into some problems and I can't get back until tomorrow. Leroy says you want me to walk you through this."

"Yes, sir. You understand I've never done this before." She tried not to let her fear show in front of the others.

"It'll be okay. So how about we try to save these little guys and their mama," he said. Doc was always one to go for the gold, and he'd set the bar high. She hoped it wasn't too high, because the thought of failing in front of her dad, Dylan, and the others terrified her.

"Okay." She let out a huge breath. She was really going to do this.

Step by step, Doc instructed her what to do and what to expect, his voice doing double duty by calming her nerves. Sweat dripped from her face to her shirt. This would be messy, and grueling, but she was as ready as she ever would be.

A shaft of light flickered briefly across the floor. Kayla looked up to see Derek and her mother walk in.

Kayla shot Dylan a pleading look. It was bad enough everyone here would witness the failure, but to have Derek lose faith in her would be the final cross to bear. He'd been through enough, and she didn't want to be the one to expose him to the pain of death again, especially by her own hand.

Dylan met her gaze but didn't acknowledge her silent request. Instead, he moved to put his hand on Derek's shoulder, a silent look of understanding passing between the two. She had no idea what it was about, but she had to trust Dylan knew best. And she needed to stay focused.

She gave an extra tug on the calf's hind legs and pulled. Finally, she felt the calf slide into the proper position. She had no idea how much time had passed, but if she had to guess, she'd say an eternity. "He's in place," she said. She'd done it. Now to go for the gold.

"I need help, someone."

Dylan stepped forward, his body pressed close. The essence of cow fetus and aftershave didn't mix, and she knew which one she preferred.

"Help the calf as he comes out," she said.

Dylan reached for the cow. "Let me pull, and you make sure the calf is okay. You need to save your strength for the next one."

"Thanks." She smiled as she withdrew her arm. She was grateful for his help and his concern, because fatigue was beginning to set in.

Dylan's strong arm replaced hers, and he pulled the calf out more gently than she would have thought possible. The calf slid out onto the straw and started to move. "He's alive," she cried, tears streaming down her face. Soft cheers echoed through the barn.

"You were wonderful," Dylan said, his deep voice filled with awe. "Congratulations. You've just delivered your first calf."

Kayla wiped the calf down to clean him off a little before moving him to a pile of hay by the mother's head, letting the cow's motherly instincts do what was best for the newborn. It was an exhilarating, tense, incredible moment. One Kayla would never forget.

"Great job, Kayla, you're hired," Doc said. "But now you've got another one to deliver. The good news is the second one is usually a whole lot easier. The second one should already be in the correct position. Give the cow about five minutes to recover and then help the other calf out if he needs it. You can call me if you run into trouble, but I think you've got this. Well done, young lady."

"Thanks, Doc. I couldn't have done it without you." This had to be the single greatest moment in her veterinary experience.

"That was awesome, Kayla," Derek said, coming to stand next to her.

She put an arm around him and hugged the boy's slender body to her own. "Thanks. I couldn't agree with you more."

"Nicely done, honey. Your mom and I are proud of you." Her parents' lingering hug spoke volumes.

"Thanks. It was spectacular, but it's not over yet. At least Doc said the second one is easier, and I'm all for easy after the first one." She laughed.

The somber mood in the barn had lifted, and in its place, rejoicing, but now it was time to finish what she started. Her confidence had grown and this time, she went straight to work.

She donned a new pair of sterile gloves. "Time for round two."

"I'm right here with you," Dylan said, his smile tugging at her heart.

"Thanks." For now, all their history was exactly that, history. Right now, they were performing a miracle together. She shouldn't like the sound of it, but she did. *Together.*

She reached in and pulled the calf forward, making sure he was in position before trading places with Dylan. Doc was right. The second one was easier.

"Ready?" he asked.

"Let's do this." The calf slid out onto the straw. Only this time the calf wasn't moving. Kayla looked on in alarm. He wasn't breathing. Rubbing the calf briskly with the towel, she looked up at Leroy.

"Get Doc on the phone," she hollered.

She felt the calf's chest for a heartbeat. A soft, faint beat pulsated against her fingertips.

"The Doc's line is busy. We're still trying," Leroy called out.

The calf would suffocate if she didn't do something.

Dylan grabbed him by his hind legs and lifted him slightly off the ground. "Leroy, massage his sides. Kayla, check for mucus in his nose and mouth."

"Nothing," she said. The calf still didn't move. Kayla's heart was breaking for the little guy.

Dylan laid the calf back on the ground. "I've seen the Doc do a little straw trick before. It's worth a try," Dylan said, kneeling down next to her. He grabbed a piece of straw and pushed it into one of the calf's nostrils. Kayla remembered reading something about the move in one of her textbooks.

She pushed his hand aside and leaned down close to the calf's head. Covering the animal's mouth with one hand and a nostril with the other, she blew gently into the open nostril. She did this for the longest, most excruciating seconds of her life before the calf coughed. And coughed again. The calf's eyes opened and looked straight at Kayla as if to say thank you. For the second time that day, she beheld the miracle of life in her arms as she hugged the calf. Tears of joy ran unchecked down her face.

"That was amazing," Dylan said. He wrapped his arm around her shoulder and drew her close, laughing at the calf struggling to move.

They needed to move the calf closer to his mother's head so she could give the calf a little motherly TLC, but for a few seconds, Kayla didn't move. She wanted to enjoy the closeness with Dylan. It might be wrong, but it felt oh so right.

After several rounds of congratulations, the ranch hands began to clean the area and Kayla finished washing up. The adrenaline in her body was subsiding, leaving her exhausted in the aftermath. It had been a life-changing experience, the second one in her life. Dylan's kiss had been the first.

"Can I give you a lift to the house?" Dylan asked.

"Mom and Dad are here. I should probably go with them. Or I could walk." Spending a few more minutes with Dylan would have been nice, but it wouldn't do her any good. Things were hard enough.

"You're too tired to walk even if it's only a short distance. Hey, Lou, mind if I give Kayla a ride back to the house?" he called out, disregarding her answer.

"Not at all. See you back home, Kayla," her dad said.

"Not exactly what I had in mind." Kayla frowned. Dylan hadn't changed much. Still the same old bossy boy he used to be, only older. And more handsome.

"I want a few minutes to talk to you."

"Okay."

"Hey, Derek, how about keeping an eye on the calves while I talk to Kayla? Let us know if anything changes." Derek's chin rose a notch, the smile on his face telling. Dylan's trust in him meant the world to the kid.

"So talk," she said, climbing into his old Ford.

He started the truck and turned on the air conditioner. The cool air felt great against her sweat-soaked clothes, sending chills across her skin.

"I'm sorry about what I said earlier. There's no excuse. I know you wouldn't turn your back on helping an animal to spite me. I felt helpless. It's not a feeling I experience often."

"I understand. If it's any consolation, I felt pretty helpless back there, too." A common bond shared between friends signaling a change in their relationship once again. Could they be friends? Or was it simply an illusion because of the experience they shared?

"You know, I think everyone, me included, thought one day you would come home when you finished school and go into practice here. Guess we thought wrong. Those city folks are mighty lucky to have you."

"I couldn't come back," she said softly. They were treading into dangerous waters.

"Why?" One simple word, but it was a question she wasn't prepared to discuss. Not now. Probably not ever. It hurt too much.

"Things happened that changed everything."

"Like me. I never planned on sticking around, either. I had my big dreams, and the next thing you know, I'm parenting Derek. It's been tough, but I don't regret it." Dylan pulled up to the house and put the truck in park. The cab grew smaller as he turned his body toward her.

"You knew I never planned on sticking around Riverbend, so it shouldn't come as a surprise to anyone really," she said.

"I guess they always thought we'd end up together."

Kayla couldn't believe what he was saying. If it wasn't so damn heartbreaking, it would be funny. "Well then, they thought wrong." She forced the words from between her lips.

"Any chance we can be friends again? I miss my little tagalong," Dylan said, reaching out to give her shoulder a playful push.

"Dylan, I can't." He didn't understand. Maybe if she explained it to him, he'd quit asking.

"I know you were going to leave Wednesday, but can you at least stay a few extra days to keep an eye on the calves?"

Dylan had zeroed in on her Achilles' heel.

"Yeah. For the calves, I'll stay a few extra days," she said, grateful for a chance to lighten the mood in the truck.

And while she was at it, she still had to go into town to talk to some people about a mechanical pivot irrigation system for the farm. Because nothing else had changed between them, and Dylan still needed to move his cows off her father's farm.

Chapter Ten

Kayla wiped the sweat off her brow. It wasn't even noon yet, and she was already drenched in sweat. Her T-shirt sported several darkened patches across the front, and the material in the back was plastered to her skin. Not overly attractive, but there wasn't a thing she could do about it as she crossed the street to Tillie's Diner.

Come lunchtime, the place should be filled with muscular, sweaty cowboys, and hopefully, a couple of them were available for hire.

She'd spent all last night working out a plan, and by nightfall hoped it would be put into action. Dylan wouldn't like it, but this wasn't about him. They may be in the middle of a truce, but saving the farm was more important than salvaging a truce with someone she should still hate.

School would be starting back soon, so time was critical. Her goal today was to line up all the details and then present it to her dad. He couldn't possibly turn down her offer to help if she could arrange it.

"Afternoon, Mr. Thompson." He hadn't changed much

since she'd last seen him, his rotund body and jovial face as sweet as the candy he used to give her at the store on the rare occasions they came to town. "I was coming to see you later, but now is good. Do you have a minute, or am I interrupting your lunch?"

"Well, if it isn't little Kayla Anderson. Does my eyes good to see you. Sit. Sit. I'd be a fool not to enjoy my lunch with a pretty companion instead of eating alone." He winked. Old coot was always an innocent flirt.

"Thanks." She slid into the seat across from him.

"What's up?" he asked after the server took their order.

"I want to pump the river water up to my dad's fields, but I need an irrigation wheelhouse, a pump, and a few hard-bodied cowboys looking to make a few extra dollars. Can you help me locate the parts and direct me to a few good cowboys needing work?"

"Those parts aren't cheap, little lady."

"I know. But my grandmother left me a small emergency nest egg, and I need to help my dad."

"I heard Dylan's cows are grazing out by the river. I'm not sure there would be enough water from the allocation to make it worth your while," he said.

"You're right. There's not. I've already told him he has to move them, because I'm taking back our rights to the water allocation." It really wasn't any of his business, but old man Thompson was her link to getting a wheelhouse. Around here, being nice was the only way to get things done if you needed help.

"Oh. And how'd he take it?"

"I didn't give him a chance to respond. Sometimes it's easier with Dylan not to let him get a word in edgewise. He could talk a coon out of his fur coat if given a chance."

Mr. Thompson threw his head back, guffawing loud enough to cause several heads to turn. It was as true as it was funny.

"You may be right there, child. He's a smart man. Stepped up and done right by the boy. I'm sure his father would be proud. Dylan knows what he wants and how to get it." Someone else singing Dylan's praises. Would the list of staunch supporters never end? The guy had a skeleton in his closet that would shock the good townspeople. Maybe then he would come down a notch or two in their high opinion.

"That's not always a good thing," she said, speaking from experience. "Do you think you can find me a wheelhouse on such short notice?"

"I'm sorry, Kayla, but the closest one I could get my hands on right now is probably over five hundred miles away. We're in the middle of a drought, and that kind of equipment gets grabbed up pretty quickly."

His answer wasn't what she wanted to hear. "But there has to be one someplace. Used would be better." Without a wheelhouse, her plan wouldn't work. Her father wouldn't admit it, but Kayla was sure he was on the verge of losing the farm.

"I can check around for you, but don't hold your breath," he said. Mr. Thompson opened his mouth to say something else, but closed it without another word, only shaking his head from side to side.

"What is it? Did you think of something?"

"No. Nothing my business to mention." He sat back in his chair and wiped his mouth with the napkin.

Odd thing to say, but whatever. "Okay, thanks. In case you find one, can you recommend anyone to do the work? I need to move on this pretty fast."

He cast her a long, assessing look before he let out a deep sigh. "Well, there's the Johnson boys, who should be in here in a little bit. And then there's Andrew, you remember Willie Tannin's son? And maybe Clifton Casey would be looking for work. You be sure to tell them where you're looking to have the work done."

Anyone from around here would know it was for the Anderson farm. Maybe old Mr. Thompson was becoming a bit senile. "Okay. Thanks a million. You're the best." She smiled.

"Your daddy know what you're trying to do?" he asked, sticking a toothpick in his mouth to chew on.

"Well, no. At least not yet. He's not keen on my help, so I wanted to see if it was feasible before told him my plan."

"Hmmm. I wondered as much. You know, sometimes you gotta let a man do what he feels he needs to do and not second guess him."

"What do you mean?" she asked.

"Seems to me your daddy would have done this already if he could, don't you think?"

"Times are tough. I can help. What kind of a daughter would I be if I didn't try to help?" The kind who hadn't hung around much for the past five years. The kind who'd been caught up in her own dreams when the tough times started.

"You have a big heart, darling. Don't mind an old fool like me. But talk to your daddy first, before we start ordering expensive parts to be hauled in. Trust me on this," he said, reaching out to pat her hand.

"Okay. I'll talk to him tonight after I see if I can round up a few guys to dig the trenches to pump the water up to the reservoir."

"Hmmph," he grunted. "Know anyone out your way who needs a dog? We're asking around trying to help old Mrs. Kimble out. Her nephew done left her with a year-old mutt she can't control or keep."

"No. Sorry. I'm heading back to the city next weekend, and I can't keep a dog in my apartment."

"No problem. I'm sure we'll find it a home. Sweet dog.

Just the right size to make some young boy or girl a nice pal, I reckon, with a little training," he added with a grin.

An image of Derek came to mind. He was upset she was leaving, but what if she left him with a new friend? Dylan didn't know everything, and maybe Kayla could talk to him, convince him to see a dog was the perfect answer to Derek's issues. Having a dog by his side would break the loneliness of the ranch, and it could teach him some responsibility. It was the perfect solution. The more she thought about it, the more she liked the idea. Maybe it was time Dylan didn't get his way.

"I have an idea. I know someone who could use a dog." The words were out before she could stop them. It felt right even if she would be overstepping her bounds. Maybe, just maybe, she could pull this off. For Derek's sake. After all, Dylan owed her one.

"I was hoping you'd think of someone." He laughed, grinning like the devil.

"Why, you, old coot, you planted the seed on purpose."

"If anyone can talk Dylan into letting Derek get a dog, I have a feeling it'll be you."

Played by a pro. "I'll do one better. Instead of talking first, I'll take the dog with me." Kayla laughed. It would serve Dylan right.

"Come by the store when you finish up in town and see what you think. If you want to take him with you, it'd be great. But if Dylan says no, you bring the dog back."

Sounded fair. "No worries." But she intended to make sure Dylan didn't say no.

"Lunch is on me," he said, rising to his feet and throwing some money on the table. "I'll see you in a few."

"Thanks. I'll be there after I talk to the guys you mentioned."

She didn't have to wait long. Andy, Cliff, and the Johnson

boys showed up at the diner about the same time. Easy smiles, loud, and charming, they stopped to say hello to several patrons. In a small town, everyone knew everyone.

Twenty minutes later, she left the diner feeling unsettled. The guys were excited to see her and quick to flirt, but not a one of them would commit to helping her out. Between the strange looks and comments from the guys and Mr. Thompson, she had a feeling she was being snowballed. Was it because she was a woman no one would help or take her serious? Or was it because her father owned the land and no one would lift a finger or commit without his approval?

She didn't relish the discussion with her dad. When it came to the property, he could be obstinate. Bottom line, he hadn't asked for her help, and he might not want it.

Kayla pulled the truck up to park in front of the hardware store. The bell above the door tinkled as she entered. She spotted Mr. Thompson right away at the register counter. "I'm here for the dog, like I promised."

"Hang on and let me get the little fellow." He went out through the swinging half door that led to the back room. While she waited, Kayla found the nutrient-rich additive she wanted to try to bottle-feed the calves in addition to their mother's milk. It would help boost their energy and help the cow since she was feeding two. Kayla was determined to do everything she could to ensure the little guys survived.

When the half door swung back open, Mr. Thompson reappeared with the cutest dog she'd ever seen. The dog pulled excitedly at his leash, trying to come say hello to the newcomer. A cross between a beagle and a Lab was her best guess. His cute little brown and white face with a black eye patch reminded her of a pirate. The high-spirited mutt wanted nothing more than attention and someone to pet him. She bent down to keep him from jumping. "Sit," she commanded. And to her surprise, he sat.

"I said he needed training, not that he didn't have any." Mr. Thompson chuckled. "His name is Patches. Not hard to figure out why."

"He's adorable." The dog licked her hand as if he understood her words. She leaned down to nuzzle his face, kissing the side of his head. "I'd keep you for myself if I could, but the city's no place for you."

"I'll be right back," Mr. Thompson said, moving off to help another customer.

Kayla laughed and played with the dog for several minutes, loving the attention the dog seemed all too happy to lavish on her. She'd have to be careful, or she'd fall for his sweet face and doggy licks.

Mr. Thompson returned, and Kayla was more than ready to take the dog with her. "I'll take him. I also need the nutrient additive I put on the counter. It's for a couple of calves over at Dylan's place."

"I heard what you done last night. Right nice of you. Heard it was a true miracle how you saved all three animals. Supplement is on me, no charge."

This she hadn't expected. Another example of small-town living she'd forgotten. His words embarrassed her. "Word travels fast," she mumbled. "I did what I could to help, even though I was scared to death."

"Sometimes things have a way of working out exactly as they are meant to be."

"Thanks. And thanks for the supplement. It's sweet of you."

"Least I could do. Here, let me carry this out since you got your hands full with Patches."

"I won't argue," she said. Patches jumped excitedly when she stood. One of the first habits Derek would need to break.

"You know, old Doc isn't getting any younger, and I reckon he could use a hand. Might be nice if he had someone like you to take his place when he retires." Mr. Thompson delivered the comment as casually as if he was talking about the weather.

Kayla opened the truck door to let Patches jump inside.

"I'm studying to be a small-animal vet, and Riverbend already has one of those. A young one, I might add. There's no place for me here." It was the easiest explanation. Anything else was far more complicated than she was willing to tell anyone.

"Seems to me you're a mixed breed now. Just like this here dog you fell in love with the instant you laid eyes on him. The town would love you, too, if you give them a chance and come home."

"My home is in the city, and the clinic there wants to take me on as a partner when I'm licensed," she said, her voice tight. Why did everyone keep making comments like her life in the city was temporary?

"Nothing's been planted that can't be replanted. Keep that in mind, will you?" Again with the cryptic comments. They were starting to get on her nerves.

"Later, Mr. Thompson," she said. It was easier to ignore his remark, and she wasn't sure how to answer it anyway.

The trip home was not the easiest with Patches trying to ride in her lap, but it sure was fun. Kayla hugged the dog before opening the door to let him out. She held on to his leash, not wanting to have him run off and get into trouble before she paved the way for his arrival.

If her timing was right, Derek should be home from school and Dylan would be out on the ranch somewhere. As long as he wasn't at the house, it would work for her. She was a little nervous about her decision, but she was willing to face the challenge head on, hoping it didn't turn into a firing squad.

Giving the dog to Derek first was blackmail, but Kayla

saw the way Dylan looked at Derek when he thought no one was watching.

Dylan loved his brother, and she hoped it would be impossible for him to resist the bit of sunshine Patches could bring into Derek's life. Kayla said a silent prayer it would all work out, because the last thing she wanted to do was upset the kid.

Patches pulled on the leash, trying his darnedest to reach the new smells assailing him all at once, his sense of curiosity and excitement kicking into overdrive. Kayla knocked on the door and waited. She let out a sigh of relief when it was Derek who opened the door.

He stepped out onto the porch, an ear-to-ear grin creasing his face.

"Hey, boy," he said, kneeling to pet the dog.

"Hey to you, too," Kayla said when Derek ignored her.

"Sorry. Hi." His gaze went right back to the dog. "When did you get him?"

Derek sat down on the porch, and Patches jumped into his lap, licking his face. The two roughhoused like old friends.

"I didn't actually get a dog. What do you think of him?"

"He's awesome. I like the goofy eye patch. Reminds me of a pirate. What's his name?"

"Patches."

"Fits, I guess." He laughed. "Hey, Patches. You're a good boy, aren't you?" He talked to the dog like he was a little kid.

"If he ain't yours, whatcha doing with him?" Derek looked up at her, curiosity in his big brown eyes.

"He needs a home, and I had an idea to bring him along."

"You thinking of keeping him?" he asked, his hand absently rubbing the dog who now sat contentedly next to him, his face planted in Derek's lap.

"I was thinking more about you."

Derek's eyes lit up with excitement but just as quickly the

light vanished.

"Dylan won't let me have a dog. I told you, I asked before, and he said no." Derek wrapped his arm tightly around the dog, pulling him close to his chest.

"Why don't you let me talk to Dylan? That is, if you think you'd want him?"

"I want him. He's awesome and he likes me," Derek said. "Would you really ask Dylan for me? No one's ever done that before. Like stood up for me."

Who could resist such a pitiful plea? No matter what Dylan decided, it was worth the risk to ask.

"I will, but there are conditions. First, he would be your responsibility. Feeding, bathing, buying food, paying his vet bills." If she was going to have a shot at this, she had to beat Dylan. He was a master at getting what he wanted, but he was about to meet his match.

"Um, I don't have a job. How could I pay for his stuff? I knew this wouldn't work." He looked like he'd lost his best friend and was about to cry.

Kayla took pity on him, but it was important she get the message across if this was going to work. "You're thirteen, aren't you?"

"Yeah."

"Well then, I would think if you do all your chores, Dylan would work out an allowance that would cover most of the expenses. And I bet he might even be willing to help you with some of the costs provided you do all your chores and all the work for the dog."

"I can do that," he answered with confidence. Kayla believed him. Now she had to make Dylan a believer.

"But no playing with the dog until your chores and homework are done. Is it a deal?"

"Do you hear that, Patches, you're gonna be my dog and live with me."

"Do we have a deal?" she asked him again.

"Hell, yeah."

"Pardon me," she said in mock horror.

"Sorry. I meant heck, yeah." At least he had the good grace to look like he meant the apology.

"That's better. It's important to learn your manners."

"Yes, ma'am," he said, smiling again.

He was a good kid who needed a little guidance. She didn't blame Dylan for his shortcomings. Running a ranch and raising a kid all by himself must be next to impossible, but it looked as if he was managing. It would have made his life a whole lot easier if he'd married Becky, not to mention he could have raised his son here.

Kayla laid out the plan with Derek, who proved he could be an avid listener when he wanted. With so much at stake, he was willing to do anything to make it work. She could tell he wasn't convinced Dylan would agree, but if he was more than willing to give it his best shot, then so was she.

"Think you can keep an eye on him until this is settled? I need to run to the barn. If you can find a long rope, it might be easier to tie him up out front to keep track of him until he becomes accustomed to you and the house."

"Gotcha. And, Kayla," he said, his boot scuffing at the ground, "thanks. Even if it doesn't work, it's nice you tried for me."

"It'll be fine, partner." If only she could be sure.

Kayla grabbed the nutrient mix from the truck and headed to the barn to check on the calves. The familiar smells of the barn evoked memories of last night's miracle. She made her way to the stall and watched as the two calves suckled on the cow's teats hungrily.

So much sweetness. Such innocence. Velvety fur covered the calves, their hide mostly white but with a few small black patches to decorate their bodies, reminding her of Patches.

She mixed the nutrient additive with some warm water and offered it in a bottle to one of the calves, but he rejected it in favor of his mother's milk. Kayla sat Indian style on the floor next to the second calf, before offering him the bottle, hoping a better position would help things along.

When the calf started to suckle the bottle, Kayla's heart exploded with love for the little guy. It was almost too much like feeding a baby. And she liked it. Babies weren't in her future, but still, it was nice. More than nice. She closed her eyes, relishing the moment.

The barn door scraped open.

"Kayla, you in here?" Dylan called out.

"Over here," she answered. She drew in a deep breath to calm her sudden nerves.

Dylan stopped outside the stall and watched her. "I saw your truck and figured I'd find you here. How's he doing?"

"This one took some nutrient milk and looks great. The other one looks good, but I'll feel better if he drinks a little from the bottle."

"I'm sure you'll get him to drink. You look like a natural. Are you sure you don't have experience with cattle you're hiding from us? Or maybe you have a secret kid stashed somewhere?" He smiled.

Kayla gasped in shock. She closed her eyes to fight the gut-wrenching pain that knifed through her body.

"Kayla, what is it? What did I say?"

She turned away, not wanting him to see her face.

"Nothing," she squeaked out. "Why haven't you ever gotten married?" She asked the first thing that came to mind, anything not to have to explain her reaction to his words.

"Whoa. Talk about a change of subject. Where did that come from?"

"I was thinking about it earlier. It would have been easier for you with Derek if you'd gotten married."

"Can't."

"Can't or won't?" she asked, digging deeper to understand Dylan and to move further from the subject locked deep in her heart and soul.

He seemed to relax with her explanation. "It doesn't matter. But lots of reasons, I guess. Between Derek and the ranch, I've never had time to invest in a relationship, and I didn't have anything to offer. I needed to rebuild the ranch, make it a place a woman would want to come home to, and more importantly, a place to stay, I reckon."

"By the looks of things, you've done all right. Derek needs a woman's influence."

"I think we've done fine." He shrugged.

"I agree. I'm not criticizing you. It's simply an observation."

"The wrong woman would be as detrimental as no woman." Was he talking about Becky? Or her?

"I agree with you there. He's a good kid."

"You wouldn't know it from his teachers lately, or even here at home. I don't know what ails him, but I'm guessing a little hard work and strict rules will keep him on the right track. Same thing my dad did for me." Dylan crossed his arms as if challenging her to disagree.

"And yet you wanted to leave." The words slipped out before she could stop them.

"Cripes, Kayla. That's low." She hadn't meant them to sound judgmental, but Dylan needed to face the past and remember what it was like being a boy growing up on the ranch.

"It's the truth. Maybe it's time to change your way of thinking."

"You have no idea what it's like. You left everything behind and never looked back. You don't know the meaning of responsibility in my world, so don't think you can preach to me or criticize what I do with my brother." The angry glint in his eyes didn't bode well for the next conversation.

"Don't go there. Just because I got out and you couldn't, doesn't mean you have the right to judge what I do, either. And I'm not preaching, merely offering an observation."

She stood there facing him, squared off, toe-to-toe, unwilling to back down. Kayla wasn't the scared teenager she'd been the last time she ran away from Dylan. Life had dealt her a double blow, and her recovery made her stronger.

"Around here, we call that meddling," he said.

"I'm only trying to help. Surely you still know what it is to dream for bigger things?"

"I do. What I want is so close I can finally taste it after all these years, but I realize I was a fool to think I could ever be good enough to get it. Life is full of disappointment, and Derek needs to learn it like the rest of us."

"Well then, I guess I just handed you his next life lesson."

Poor Derek. Kayla didn't stand a chance of convincing Dylan. Maybe it would have been better to talk to him first. The way he was acting now, he would go ballistic when he found out what she'd done.

"What the hell does that mean?" he asked, his voice low and demanding.

"You're a hard and overbearing brute sometimes. Someone who can't see past his own disappointment to figure out the power of love works better than the power of rules."

"What have you done?" Dylan glared at her.

"I got Derek a dog." No pretty speeches. No convincing plan. The plain truth.

"What?" he yelled in disbelief, a thunderous look on his face.

"You heard me. I brought him a dog who needs a home as much as Derek needs a dog. They're up at the house playing as we speak."

"Who the hell do you think you are? You can't swoop in here, make a mess of everything, and then walk away. He already hates me enough without you stirring up trouble." Dylan turned and started to walk away.

She wasn't backing down, and she wasn't letting him walk away from her again without an explanation. "Why not? I deserve an answer. You walked away once before and left my life in a mess." Her words stopped him in his tracks.

He spun back around. "Are you serious? I saved your life. I kept you from being stuck in a town you hated. You can't even begin to compare it to this," he growled. "You didn't even bother to ask me first because you knew I would say no." Dylan closed the distance between them. "And do you know why I would say no? It's because an untrained dog can be a hazard around cattle and stir up trouble. It's because Derek can barely do his homework and chores. It's because my hands are already full with everything else I need to do around here. Where do you get off thinking he can handle a dog?"

"Maybe it's time to find out. Maybe he needs a friend. Maybe it's exactly what he needs in his life at this exact moment to get him back on track."

"The answer is no. You don't know him the way I do. And you're going to be the one to tell him."

Like hell she would. Maybe if he'd been nicer they could have talked it over, but this was total bull. "I won't do it. I'm leaving. I'll be back tomorrow to check on the calves."

"Kayla, I'm warning you. Get the dog and tell Derek you changed your mind."

"Tell him yourself, Mr. Heartless. But hear him out before you tear them apart. You can return the dog to Mr. Thompson if you still feel the need. Or better yet, I can pick up the dog in the morning. Patches is a great dog who needs a little love in his life, too. Something you obviously don't understand."

Chapter Eleven

He couldn't believe Kayla had dumped the whole dog crisis on his head, but the early morning barking coming from Derek's room was a stark reminder. She had no right to interfere in something she knew nothing about, but she'd played her hand well. Round one went to Kayla.

The minute he'd laid eyes on Derek and the dog playing happily in the front yard, Dylan knew it was too late. The damage had already been done. His brother was hooked, and he *would* be the heartless jerk Kayla accused him of being if he took the dog away. It was an underhanded move on her part, and there was nothing he hated more than having someone force his hand to accept something he knew would end badly.

Dylan relented, but only for the time being. Patches would have to prove his place on the ranch, something not all dogs were cut out to do. A lesson Dylan had learned the hard way.

High-strung and eager for action, Patches reminded him of his dog Buster. They'd been inseparable, or at least they had been until the day Buster had been trampled by a herd of stampeding cattle.

His father claimed Buster had spooked the herd, but Dylan never believed it. Either way, it didn't matter. Dylan had been forced to bury Buster. From that day forward, he couldn't wait to get the hell out of Riverbend and far, far away from the ranch.

The irony of the situation still had the power to reach deep into his soul and twist his insides with its deathlike grip. It was Buster's death that had driven Dylan to want to escape, but it was his parents' deaths that had shackled him to stay.

There was no way to know how this would end for Derek, but Dylan would be there to help him pick up the pieces if it didn't work out. Contrary to Kayla's accusations, he was far from heartless.

Heartless would have been leaving Derek with their aunt and uncle in the city, and heartless wouldn't have let Kayla walk away. No, he wasn't heartless by a long shot.

"Derek, get up, lazy bones." The dog turned his head to see who'd come into the room before he curled back up next to Derek. It was as if the dog sensed Dylan didn't want him around. A dog in bed was another big rule breaker, but it was a rule Dylan had managed to break quite a few times when he used to sneak Buster in late at night. It was the first time he thought of Buster without an ache in his heart. Patches was a good-looking dog, and Derek had fallen hard.

"What time is it?" Derek mumbled. His arm came out from beneath the blankets and wrapped around Patches to snuggle the dog closer.

Dylan's heart melted a little more. "Time for you to get up and get your morning chores done, which now include the dog, I might add. It's what you promised."

"But it's only four thirty," he groaned.

"Welcome to your new world. It's called responsibility. A

deal's a deal."

"Yes, sir," he mumbled groggily, swinging his legs to the side of the bed.

Dylan was impressed, not only by the "sir", but by the fact Derek was moving. It probably wouldn't last, but it was a nice change. And when his brother got off to school on time and left the dog tied up out front as instructed, Dylan was bowled over.

He'd spent the morning working on one of the fences, returning to the house when it was time to meet up with Leroy. With a few extra minutes to spare, he stopped in to check on Patches.

He laughed when the dog lifted his head, a pleading look in his puppy-dog eyes. Written in the laws of inevitability, a dog tied to a rope near any immovable object, the dog would become wrapped around the object. He stooped down to pat the dog on the head.

"There, there, boy. I'll take care of you."

Dylan untied the rope from his collar, an action made more difficult with each lap of wet doggy tongue across his hands.

"Yeah, I know. Being tied up stinks. But until you learn your way around, it's safer. We wouldn't want you getting hurt and breaking Derek's heart, now would we?"

He picked up a stick from nearby and threw it. "Fetch, boy," he commanded. The dog jumped and barked, running after the stick, and pounced on it. Patches lay down across half the stick and began chewing on the other half.

Fetch obviously hadn't been a part of his training.

"I hope you're a good dog, because I wouldn't mind keeping you around. You bring back bittersweet memories for me, but I reckon it's time they were replaced."

The dog returned to his side and rubbed his head against Dylan's knee, as if he understood.

"But don't tell anyone. Let's keep it as our little secret. Okay, Patches?"

He needed to get going but stayed and watched the dog a few more minutes before reluctantly retying him. "I'll be back to check on you a little later. Try to stay out of trouble this time," he said, refilling the water bowl. Walking away, he could hear Patches barking. It was almost impossible not to turn around and go back, but he had work to do, and it didn't include being hampered by a dog who could cause more trouble than help.

"Hey there," Kayla said from behind him. He spun around in time to see her grinning, a far cry from last night's parting expression.

They both knew damn well why she was grinning. "Morning. Calves are looking good," he said, hoping to avoid any conversation about the dog. Last night had been enough.

"Thanks," she said.

"For what?"

"Keeping the dog. Giving him a chance. You won't be sorry."

A man could get used to waking up next to her radiant smile, not to mention the rest of her perfectly delectable body. She was dressed in tight blue jeans and a T-shirt, and Dylan felt the pull of attraction hit him square in the gut.

"I hope you're right," he said, trying to tamp down the desire to pull her in his arms and kiss her.

"What changed your mind?" she asked. Her smile deepened, if it were possible.

"You. Mr. Heartless was a bit heavy handed, but not nearly as heavy handed as conspiring with a thirteen-year-old to counter any argument. Well played." Dylan removed his hat and tipped his head in a sweeping gesture to acknowledge her win.

"Deep down, you're a softie, but you try to keep it hidden.

It's okay to show the world who you are and what you want. And when you hurt. I know this is about Buster."

"You're wrong. Men are expected to be tough and strong. Any sign of weakness, and you lose respect. You wouldn't understand." This wasn't the conversation he expected to be having with Kayla.

"You never talked about him after he died. And as far as I know, you've never had another dog. Maybe it's time to let another dog in your life. It could be great for you both."

She could save her psychoanalysis for her city friends, especially since her words hit too close to home. "Hmmphh," he said gruffly. "You here to check on the calves?"

"I've got some more colostrum for them. Hopefully, I can get them both to drink today. Doc said it's safer and there's a lower rate of mortality if I can do the supplements for at least the first four days."

"Sounds good to me. I appreciate you sticking around and agreeing to help take care of them. I'm two hands down while they are away visiting family, so everyone's already overloaded."

"No problem." She moved into the corral and knelt next to the first calf, stroking his silky fur to help him relax. She glanced up at Dylan, her brow furrowed.

"You going to stand here and watch?" she asked.

"I'm supposed to meet Leroy, but, yeah, for now, I'll watch."

The sight of her feeding the calf struck a chord in him. Soft, sweet, and motherly, the light in her eyes as she held the bottle to the calf's mouth was riveting. Being a veterinarian was her calling, but Dylan couldn't help but wonder how she would look with a baby in her arms. His baby.

If he had a second chance with her, she would always come first.

"You should get going. I can handle this. I promise."

"Maybe I like watching you better." He knew she was off-limits, but it didn't stop his mouth from uttering the words in his heart.

"Dylan, please." A frown tugged at the corners of her mouth.

"No harm in stating the truth."

"Never mind. But if you're going to stand there watching, you're going to have to talk to me. Tell me how things are going."

"Okay. I can do that much." He chuckled. If she wanted him to talk, he'd talk. It was a good opportunity to try and explain a few things to her while she couldn't run away.

"It's tough around here. This is the third year in a row we've had drought conditions, and it's been tough for everyone. When I bought the cattle with the insurance money after my dad died, I also had several reservoirs built to combat the effects of a drought. Not much can protect you three years in a row without a major source of natural ground water running through the property. That's why the cattle are grazing down by the river. It was either that or sell the herd at rock-bottom prices to save the ranch. I guess what I'm trying to explain is things have been rough for everyone, your dad included."

She glanced up at him, her brow drawn tight. "You still have to move the cattle. I'm planning on having an irrigation system installed as soon as Mr. Thompson can locate a wheelhouse for me. Dad needs the water, and I'm not trying to be mean, but they are his water allocations. You'll need to transport water in until the drought breaks."

"Thirty thousand gallons of it? It's not realistic. Besides, your dad and I have an arrangement, and at this point, it's between him and me."

"The farm is my business. It's my home."

Music to Dylan's ears even if the words to the song were

a bit garbled.

"It's your business if you move back home to stay. Otherwise, your home is in Houston," he said.

"Someone has to look out for my parents." She moved to the second calf to repeat the process.

"Your folks are pretty sharp. They know exactly what they're doing."

The calf seemed to sense Kayla's mood and turned away, looking for his mother.

"Letting the crop die out? That's a tough sell," she said in total disbelief.

"Or maybe you could trust them?"

"Or maybe you could let me figure out what's best for my own parents?"

"Like you let me figure out what's best for Derek?" he countered. The shot scored.

"Touché."

He needed to work, and the poor calf needed to take the bottle. Leaving was best all the way around now. "I've gotta go, and that poor calf needs more of your undivided attention," he said.

Stopping a few feet away, he turned back. "Any chance you want to come for dinner to see Derek and Patches tonight?" *And me.* But it was better at this point if she didn't know all his motives. Just because she'd accepted the partnership didn't mean she couldn't change her mind.

"I shouldn't. Things are complicated enough." Her head was tilted to one side while she gnawed on her lower lip.

"What's complicated about seeing a boy and his dog? You said Derek needed a woman's influence in his life. Here's your chance to make good on your words. Dinner's at seven, if you dare." He added the parting shot, knowing it was hard for her to resist a challenge.

It was cheap to use his brother and the dog as a draw

card, but somewhere in the middle of the night, Dylan had decided to fight for Kayla.

It was time to cowboy up.

The afternoon dragged out, but finally it was time to fix dinner. Seven fifteen rolled around, and there was still no sign of Kayla. Dylan stirred the spaghetti sauce to keep it from sticking.

He hadn't said a word to his brother about the dinner invitation because the kid had enough disappointment to last him a lifetime without adding Kayla into the mix. Somehow, she'd been able to wade past the surface with Derek, and the changes in him this past week were nothing short of astounding. While he, on the other hand, never seemed to get it right.

Between school and the dog, he couldn't decide if he should resent her interference or be grateful, but the slight respite in his dealings with Derek had him leaning toward grateful, at least for the moment. Sooner or later, Dylan would be left to pick up the pieces when she left.

He stepped out on the porch and looked around. Happy shouts from the side of the house told him exactly where his brother and Patches could be found. Dylan rounded the corner to get their attention and pulled up short when he spotted Kayla in the mix.

The spaghetti could wait a few more minutes.

Kayla's long ponytail swished from side to side as she frolicked with the pair, full of life. Her musical laughter eased the tension from his body.

He could have stood there and watched for hours, but the spaghetti would burn on the bottom if they delayed any longer. "Dinner!"

They both stopped and turned to look his way.

"Sorry I'm a little late, but it sounds like you haven't eaten yet. Can I still join you?" she asked, walking toward him.

Hell yes. "Sure. It's spaghetti, and I always make plenty. Put the dog in your bedroom, Derek. I don't want him jumping on Kayla or begging food at the dinner table."

"Yes, sir." Dylan couldn't believe his ears. Two days in a row, and Derek was still on his best behavior.

Bouncing from subject to subject, the brothers vied for attention from the most attractive guest to ever sit down to the table. The Fearless Five and occasional ranch hand couldn't compare.

Her laughter was infectious. No small girly giggles from his country girl, and when she started to regale Derek with some of Dylan's less-than-smart childhood pranks, it didn't take long before he served her up with a dose of her own medicine and told a few tales on her also.

Several times, he caught Kayla watching him, a strange expression on her face. But then just as quickly, she'd turn away as if embarrassed at being caught. Those were the perfect moments to observe her unguarded. The last time he remembered such an enjoyable dinner had been when his mother was alive. The thought was sobering. The ranch needed a woman's touch to make it a home.

Dylan needed to tell Kayla how he felt. The rest was up to her.

"Anyone up to a walk?" Dylan suggested.

"I don't know." Kayla looked unsure of what to do.

"Please," Derek chimed in. Kayla had a soft spot for his brother, and it made Dylan a little jealous. Unreasonably so, but still jealous.

"Okay, okay." She smiled. "But not too late. We can stop at the barn and I'll check in on the calves again."

Dylan stopped at the front door to grab his hat and boots. "Son of a gun," he yelled. The tops of his boots were dark and dampened, and there was a pool of liquid around them on the floor.

"Your dog peed on my boots. I suggest you get something to clean it up before you catch up to us on the walk," he seethed.

"But they're your boots," Derek whined, moving closer to Kayla.

"And it's your dog."

Muttering under his breath, Derek wandered off in the direction of the kitchen.

"Lighten up. It's not like those boots haven't stepped in worse," Kayla teased.

"I won't have a damn dog peeing in the house. Or on my boots. A man's boots are sacred."

"If you weren't so macho male all the time, maybe he wouldn't feel the need to mark his territory." She laughed.

The dog was bad enough, but to have Kayla laughing at him was ten times worse. No, ten times better. It was like old times.

Dylan relaxed. "You're right." He chuckled. "Hope the dog's a quick learner. I'm master of this domain, and he's pretty low in the pecking order."

Dylan went to grab his hat from the back of the chair only to discover it missing. "Where the heck's my hat?"

"Maybe you wore it in the kitchen," Kayla suggested.

"Hat and boot check at the door. That way they're always exactly where I need them when I go out again." The door swung open, and Derek walked in with the cleaning supplics.

"Oh, hell. The damn dog," Dylan mumbled out loud. This wasn't going to turn out good. If Patches had been stupid enough to mess with his hat, he'd find himself relegated to the barn. Dylan walked down the hall and glanced in each room, Kayla close on his heels.

"You don't know for sure." Her voice didn't sound confident, and she wasn't laughing. Everyone knew you never, ever, messed with a cowboy's hat. It took months and months to break one in, years to make it perfect.

When they reached Derek's room, the dog sat in the middle of the floor surrounded by tattered pieces of Dylan's hat, his tail thumping the floor in excitement.

"The dog has got to go," Dylan bellowed.

Derek came running and halted when he saw the mess Patches had made of the hat. "I'm sorry, Dylan. Please don't make him go. I'll pay for a new one. Extra chores, anything, just don't make him go," Derek's voice trembled.

Kayla laid her arm on Dylan's, her touch silencing him before he could argue. "Dylan, please." Her soft, silky plea matched the feel of her hands against his skin.

The hat wasn't important compared to the two sets of pleading eyes trained on him.

"If you'd done what you were told, we wouldn't be having this problem. Keep the dog in your room when he's in the house until we can trust him, and I prefer him outside and tied up when you're not home, at least until we can get him used to the cattle."

"I'm sorry. I forgot to close the bedroom door."

"Don't let it happen again."

"Thanks, Dylan. You're the best," Derek said, his face lit up with a smile once more.

"You won't be sorry," Kayla said in a low voice. His skin burned where her hand lay on his arm. He swallowed hard, fighting against the desire threatening to overwhelm him.

Right from the start, it had been written in the stars for them to be together, and damned if he was going to let the woman he loved go without a fight. It had to be her decision to stay, but there was nothing stopping him from trying to sway her decision.

"I hope you're right. I really hope you're right." *For everyone's sake.*

. . .

Crisis averted. It was a good thing she'd gone to dinner, or Patches would have been history by morning. Trouble was, keeping the peace between the brothers would be a full-time job, and she could only stay a few more days. She had to get back before school started.

Playing cards after dinner had been almost, well, *natural*. For the space of one night, they'd managed to stay clear of cattle, droughts, farms, and ranches, all in exchange for an evening of Crazy Eights. Crazy was a word that didn't even begin to explain the experience.

Dylan's warm laughter and easy manner was reminiscent of the man she'd fallen in love with, back when she was naive and immature. But tonight, past hurts faded and an awareness she shouldn't be feeling had crept to the surface.

Derek, on the other hand, had been the life of the party with his antics, including a competitive streak that kept them playing long after dinner. Two hours longer.

The truck rumbled down the gravel driveway, the headlights bouncing with each rut she hit. The old farmhouse was still lit up, including her father's study. Fun and games over, it was time to let her dad in on her plans to save the farm.

She made her way down the hall. "Hey there," she called out from the open doorway. "You got a minute?"

Her dad looked up, a welcoming smile on his face. One that wouldn't last.

"Sure. Did you have a good time at the ranch?" His question wasn't surprising since they'd all but shoved her out the door when they discovered she was headed to Dylan's for dinner.

"Yes. The dog is a handful, but I think I managed to avert a crisis." She laughed. "The dog's great for Derek, whether

Dylan sees it or not."

"I'm not so sure you should have done it without asking, but I can't disagree with your line of thinking about Derek. The boy needed something."

"What's done is done. Besides, I would have taken the dog if Dylan said no." She'd flung the idea at Dylan without thought, but she realized it was true. The little pirate dog had won her over completely with a few wet doggy-tongue baths.

Derek had won her over as well, but she couldn't very well uproot him and take him to the city. She would miss them both. Not to mention Dylan.

"Dog that active wouldn't do well in the city, especially with the long hours I expect you work," her father said. The voice of reason. The same matter-of-fact voice he used when she was a child, but she wasn't a child anymore.

"I would have figured something out. Patches is a sweetheart."

"So what's up? I get the feeling you're not here to talk about Patches."

"Promise to hear me out before you start objecting." Her plan was good, but convincing her dad would be the tricky part. His old-school way of doing things wasn't working, and he should have installed an irrigation system years ago.

"Depends, but I'm listening." He sat back in his chair, arms folded over his chest.

"It's about the farm. I think you can save the crop if we irrigate. I have enough money to buy a wheelhouse, a pump, and to pay for the labor to install it. Old Mr. Thompson is trying to locate a wheelhouse now. When he finds one, I'll come back and oversee getting it put into place, so it doesn't add to your workload. I've talked to some of the locals in town, but everyone is too busy or flat out tells me no. I was hoping you could rustle up a couple guys, because I keep hitting a brick wall."

Her father sat there in stony silence, his gaze never wavering as she laid out the plan.

The hard look on his face meant she'd failed.

"I've heard everything you have to say, and now it's my turn. I don't want a wheelhouse, a pump, or any locals to install anything. I told you I have everything under control."

"The crop is dying. How is that having everything under control?" she asked in frustration.

"I've made arrangements with Dylan, and I'm a man of my word. Leave it alone." He leaned back in the wooden desk chair, his hands massaging his forehead.

"So unarrange it. You said yourself folks around here are losing their farms and ranches. You don't want to be one of them because of some gentleman's agreement you have with Dylan. By the looks of things, he can survive another season. I'm not so sure about the farm."

Her father's jaw tightened in anger. Kayla knew she'd crossed an unspoken line, but it had to be done.

"The farm is my business. You chose to go to the city and turn your back on your heritage. I don't see where what I do with the farm is any of your business, unless you've had a change of heart and can tell me right here and now you're moving home when you finish vet school."

She'd never heard her father sound so final. Completely void of emotion. She'd only been trying to help, and for her efforts, she'd gotten knocked down. By her own father.

"Fine. Sorry I tried to help. But whether you like it or not, I'm still a part of the family."

"Then come home where you belong, Kayla Lynn. It's not too late."

"It's not that easy anymore. Maybe once upon a time," she said, unsure how the conversation had switched to her so quickly.

"You can change anything you want."

Seeds of doubt already planted were growing like weeds in her carefully planned life. She had to put an end to the conversation.

"You know about the partnership in the clinic when I graduate. I've already accepted."

"Like I said, nothing you can't change. You should learn to listen to your heart. You belong here."

"I am. I'm sorry you don't approve." She hated the weak tremble in her voice. Her eyes glassed over with unshed tears. *You knew it would be this way all along. It's why you didn't want to tell them.*

Unfortunately, coming home had brought her face-to-face with the past and her future. And Kayla wasn't sure where she belonged anymore.

Her father let out a deep sigh. "I understand why you left, but what's keeping you from coming home?"

Time for a little honesty. "Too many memories and too much history, I guess. And the town's not big enough for another vet." She smiled gently.

"How long you gonna keep running from your heart?" he asked.

"Mom told you about Dylan, I take it?" she asked, already knowing the answer.

"He's a good man. Done well by his brother. He's a man I'd be proud to call my son, and a man worthy of your love."

Kayla knew better, although after tonight, the memories were clouded with contradiction. It wasn't fair to pin the pain associated with the miscarriage on Dylan, in all fairness, he hadn't even known about it. But it didn't change the rest of the story.

"It was history before it ever got started. Things happened that can't be undone."

Her father looked at her, one eyebrow raised in question.

"I'm not going to discuss the details, because I didn't

come into town to stir up trouble. Trust me, the past is best left to the past."

"If you say so, but I think you're making a mistake hiding in the city."

She was beginning to agree. But what else was there? A life of emptiness because the one man who'd stolen her heart had thrown it away carelessly.

"My mistake to make, though." That didn't sound right. "Not that it's a mistake," she corrected quickly.

"Whatever you decide is your business, but the farm is my business. Let's agree to disagree, on both subjects."

Chapter Twelve

The following morning, Dylan drove toward the back of the property to fix a downed section of fence he'd noticed yesterday. The truck rumbled down the dirt path, and Dylan caught himself whistling "Brown Eyed Girl." Kayla had understood him all too well the other night when he'd made a color substitute in the song, and after last night, he understood all too well what he had been missing when he let her go.

Precious gold and completely out of reach. It would be easier to hang on for an eight-second ride on the meanest bull in the county, but it was a ride he was willing to take.

He stripped off his shirt, the early morning sun already holding the promise of another scorcher day. Dylan pounded nail after nail into the fence to make the necessary repairs. Sweat dripped from his brow, blinding him. He paused to wipe his forehead with the bandana tucked in his back pocket.

The low, distant rumble of cow hooves reached his ears. Dylan swung around to scan the horizon. Off in the distance, he spotted a large herd of cattle stampeding in his direction.

Several ranch hands were gaining ground on the stampeding herd as they gave chase. Their shouts could be heard above the din of hooves as they barreled toward him.

Patches streaked out like lightning on the right side of the herd, his bark wild and excited as he nipped at their heels.

Damn dog.

This was exactly why he didn't want a dog on the ranch. History was repeating itself all over. It was Buster he saw running next to the herd. The scene replayed in his head as if it were yesterday. The herd turned and Buster never stood a chance, tumbling under the herd's giant bodies over and over. Dylan couldn't get to him and he'd never felt so helpless.

Shouts from the ranch hands reached his ears, and everything snapped back into focus.

The guys were gaining ground, forcing the herd toward the river. A slight turn to the left sent them careening in his direction. He jumped in the truck to avoid being trampled and searched for Patches. He had to save the dog. Buster. Patches. Derek. It was a mindless blur as he searched the herd for the little dog. Dylan would do anything to save Derek the gut-wrenching heartache of losing his best friend.

Leroy pushed his mount harder to get to the head of the herd and at the last second, managed to turn the herd back in the direction of the river.

Dylan spotted Patches. Thank God, he was still alive.

"Patches!" he screamed at the top of his lungs, jumping out of the truck.

The dog paused to look in his direction. "Come," he shouted.

To his surprise, the dog looked back once at the slowing herd and then back at Dylan, before finally following his command.

Grabbing Patches when he got close enough, he tossed him in the truck.

"Damn mangy mutt. This is exactly why you can't stay. I was a fool to think this would work out. Kayla was wrong, and Derek's going to have one more thing to hate me for." Dylan glared at the dog crouched in the corner, his head between his paws as if he understood every word.

"I should have never let her sweet talk me into letting you stay. You're history."

Dylan watched as the ranch hands brought the herd to a halt at the river. One of them waved to signal everything was under control. He breathed a sigh of relief.

It would break Derek's heart, but the dog had to go before the cattle, the dog, or someone else got hurt. Someone like Derek or Kayla. It was a risk he wasn't willing to take for the people he loved most in life. After school, he would have to tell Derek.

Hours later, the conversation had gone exactly as he'd expected. Derek hated him. What he hadn't expected was for his brother to immediately call Kayla for reinforcement. Standing his ground would be a hell of a lot harder with the sweet and sassy minx who unknowingly held his heart in the palm of her hand.

It wasn't long before she knocked at the door.

"Dylan, can we take a walk? Derek, you don't mind, do you?" Kayla asked.

Derek shook his head from side to side, crocodile tears in his eyes.

"I'll take a walk, but I'm not changing my mind, so you can save your breath if that's what you have planned," Dylan said.

"Don't. Not here." Her voice was like warm honey dripping over his brain.

"I'm going to my room with Patches. You two do what you want," Derek grumbled. He left the room without a backward glance, Patches close on his heels.

Dylan stepped off the porch, and the two of them walked in silence until they were well out of range of the house.

"I understand why you're angry, but dogs can be trained. He chewed through his rope. The answer is to get him a chain, not get rid of him. You're not giving Patches a real shot at fitting in here. Let Derek work with him. He loves the dog and would do anything to keep him."

"Someone could have been hurt today. He caused a stampede of over fifty head of cattle. What if it had been Derek out there working on the fence, and he didn't know what to do?" Images of the cattle stampeding toward his brother, crushing him under their massive weight filled him with horror. It was too dangerous. His father was right. There were dogs trained to herd cattle, but they weren't family pets, they were working dogs.

"In a few years, he would know what to do. And in a few years, the dog would be trained."

"This isn't the place for Patches. You need to take him home with you."

"This is about Buster, isn't it?"

Dylan scowled. "I wouldn't want Derek to go through a similar experience."

"Your experiences made you the man you are today. Is that a bad thing?"

How the hell was he supposed to answer the question? She'd twisted this angle to her benefit. She stopped walking and touched his arm casually, but there was nothing casual about the way it made him feel. Once upon a time, a long time ago, her touch had branded him. And it still held the same power.

"Dylan, give him a second chance. Let him work with the dog and train him. I know you want what's best for him, but don't you see, the dog *is* the best thing for him," she pleaded.

"If I do, will you give *me* a second chance?" he demanded.

Two could play her game. They both wanted something, and he wasn't above coercion.

"That's blackmail," she gasped.

He took a step closer and leaned down for his second taste of heaven in five years.

His arms went around her and pulled her against his body when she didn't resist. He deepened the kiss until her lips opened enough to tangle his tongue with hers. Sweet mother. She belonged to him. He could taste it in her kiss. How could he make her understand the truth of what still existed between them? Of where she belonged?

He moved his hands down to mold over her soft feminine curves, lifted his head, and was encouraged by the desire flaming in her eyes.

"Tell me there's nothing between us, and I'll let you go."

• • •

"There's nothing between us." Four impossible words ripped from the depths of her soul. Kayla saw her own pain echoed in Dylan's eyes right before he closed them. Seizing the moment, she slipped out of his arms and ran to where she left Dizzy.

She launched herself into the saddle with one swift move, ignoring Dylan as he called out. A quick flick of her heels, and her mare was off and running.

It was self-preservation that had forced the impossible words from her lips.

Dylan's kiss brought up too many memories, his words the ones she'd longed to hear from his lips. But it was too late. Too late. Too late. The words repeated in her head with each pounding hoof as they raced across the meadow.

Neither her heart nor her brain had forgotten him. The void left in the pit of her belly from his betrayal gutted her the same way it had when she was eighteen. All the running in the world hadn't changed a single thing. Dylan Hunter was the love of her life and the bane of her existence.

Tears streaked down her face, clouding her vision. Kayla gave Dizzy the lead, letting the mare run wherever her heart desired, as long as it was away from what Kayla's heart desired. Dizzy seemed to understand her need to escape perfectly.

She leaned down to hold on to the mare's long, solid neck as she galloped across the field and Kayla reveled in the freedom.

Hours later, she returned to the barn, completely exhausted. The ride had given her plenty of time to realize several things she hadn't been prepared to admit.

The country was a part of her soul, and coming back to her roots was the piece of the puzzle she'd been missing. She'd never be happy living in the city, tending to people's cats and dogs without ever really getting to know anyone. Helping birth a newborn calf had brought her more joy than all the years of training she'd been through previously. There was something about connecting with life and connecting with folks around here that felt good. Really good.

Her only problem was Dylan. She might still love him, but she wasn't sure it was enough to forgive him.

Back at the barn, Kayla picked up the curry brush and began to rub Dizzy's coat, her hands moving by memory rather than her tear-blurred vision. She swiped at the tears with the back of her hand, angry she couldn't control her emotions.

"Why, Dylan, why? How could you walk away and leave me? And what kind of man turns his back on his own son? And what does it say about me if I still love you?" she sobbed out. Dizzy couldn't answer, but the horse nuzzled her head against Kayla's shoulder as if she understood.

The barn door banged.

"Is someone there?" No one answered.

Chapter Thirteen

Derek had taken off without a word after Kayla left, so when Dylan heard the front door slam and the heavy stomping up the stairs, it was a welcome relief. It wasn't the first time Derek was in a snit, and it wouldn't be the last, but at least he had Patches to console him this time.

Except you're planning to take away his new best friend.

Kayla's words echoed through the room, over and over. Nothing a chat with Johnny Walker couldn't drown out.

But he was wrong.

Three glasses of whisky later, the only thing that had changed was the clock on the wall ticking away the minutes. If anything, Kayla's words had become a more dominant force in the room, pushing him to the edge of no return. She didn't understand. No one could understand the pain of losing your best friend. It was something he'd never shared with anyone, and Kayla had come too damn close to guessing the truth. But the truth didn't mean Dylan could handle history repeating itself.

He stood and headed for the stairs. Five a.m. came the

same time every day, no matter what time he went to bed. And tomorrow's long to-do list had one more item he hadn't planned on. Returning the dog to old Mr. Thompson.

He stopped outside Derek's door and paused for a second before turning the knob. The door creaked open, but Derek was fast asleep, Patches curled up in a tight ball at his side. The dog lifted his head to look up at Dylan, his tail thumping against the bed repeatedly to say hello.

Dylan made a move toward the bed and Patches started to rise.

"Stay," Dylan commanded.

The dog laid his head back down but continued to watch Dylan with interest.

Buster had been a great dog, but a terrible ranch dog. Maybe if he'd spent more time training him and less time trying to get out of his responsibilities by playing hooky and hanging with his friends, his dog would still be alive. It was a hard lesson, and one Dylan would never forget.

Would the outcome have been any different if his father had shown him the way?

Dylan sat down on the edge of the bed and the dog skootched toward him. Half puppy, half dog, his big black eyes looked up at him with trust. He reached out to stroke the dog's face, his palm connecting with wet tongue instead. Dylan's heart melted like ice in a pot over a fire.

The mutt had stolen his way into Dylan's heart just as assuredly as he had into Derek's. There was no way he could get rid of the dog. Patches was here to stay.

The next morning Dylan left a note for Derek on the kitchen table, he headed for town to pick up a load of feed. The note was insurance Derek wouldn't skip from school again. The kid came up with enough reasons of his own without Dylan adding to the list.

Three hours later, Dylan pulled into the driveway and

around to the barn to unload the feed. His body ached from loading the hundred-pound feed bags alone, but it had been that or wait for Mr. Thompson's son to get back from his errand to help. There was too much to be done at the ranch to wait around for anyone.

He glanced over at the side yard of the house to check on Patches but didn't see the little dog. He crossed the yard to look around, hoping he was tied up and sitting under the porch. An uneasy feeling settled in the pit of his stomach as he drew close. The chain sat in a heap by the tie down. Either Derek had forgotten to tie him up this morning, or Patches had slipped the collar, but Dylan was laying odds against his brother, because the collar was nowhere in sight.

He should have known the kid wasn't up to the responsibility.

"Patches," Dylan called out, crossing the yard. Nothing. He opened the front door, "Patches, here, boy," he called out again. Nothing.

Dylan checked the kitchen. The dog's food and water bowls were missing, as well as the bag of dog food Kayla had left.

A quick glance at the kitchen table showed no signs of Derek having eaten the cereal Dylan had poured this morning. His heart constricted when his gaze landed on the note he'd left tucked under the spoon.

Derek hadn't come down to breakfast, which meant he hadn't seen the note. He didn't know Dylan had changed his mind about Patches. *Damn. Damn. Damn.*

He took the stairs two at a time, hoping and praying his suspicions were wrong.

Dylan pushed open the door. Nothing. He raced back to the barn. "Derek! Patches!"

Thankfully, Jezebel was still in her stall. Derek couldn't have gone far.

He checked the calf stall, knowing how much Derek loved the baby calves. Nothing.

He called the school, only to find out his brother hadn't shown up today. Dylan was 99 percent sure his brother had run away.

And it was his fault.

If only he'd listened to or paid more attention to his brother. He had to find him. His parents had trusted him to do right by Derek, and he'd failed. Miserably. He called Leroy, hoping someone had spotted his brother or the dog. He hung up the phone in frustration. Another dead end.

One last call, and then he would pull out all stops, notify the sheriff, and organize a search party.

"Lou, it's Dylan. Have you seen any sign of Derek or Patches?"

"No. Sorry. Shouldn't he be at school this time of day?"

"Yes. But I got back from town and some of his things and the dog are missing. I called the school, but Derek never showed up."

"Let me look around, and I'll get back to you," Lou said, worry evident in his voice.

"Any chance they're with Kayla?" Dylan asked hopefully. Derek trusted her, and it stood to reason he would turn to her now.

"No. Sorry to have to tell you, but Kayla left town late last night."

"Left?" First Derek, and now Kayla. Everyone he loved was deserting him.

He fought back against the pain gripping his chest. He couldn't worry about her right now. She was a grown woman, old enough to make her own choices, and she didn't need him. That much was clear. But Derek needed him.

"Left as in back to the city. Said something came up at the clinic and she had to get back."

"Thanks for letting me know. I'll wait for your call to see what you find before I notify the sheriff." The next ten minutes were the longest of his life. He answered on the first ring when Lou called him back.

"Sorry, Dylan. There's no sign of him here, and I think you're right about him leaving. I found his bike in the barn, his book bag emptied of his school things, and Mary said it looks like some food is missing from the fridge along with some bottled water. I reckon you ought to be calling in for help."

"Thanks. I'll get right on it " He'd driven his brother away when he'd threatened to take away his new best friend. Dylan knew what it was like to lose a dog, and he wouldn't wish those feelings on anyone, least of all Derek. He'd been such an idiot. All along, his brother had needed him, and while he tried to do right by him, the reality was, he hadn't given him what he needed. At least nothing a boy could hold on to. No one to make him feel loved.

"Any idea why he ran? Might help us to know where to look?"

"I told him he had to get rid of the dog. I changed my mind, but he doesn't know it."

"Interesting both Kayla and Derek are running away from you. Maybe it's high time you take action and show them how you feel."

"I've tried, trust me, I've tried."

"Maybe that's the problem. You're trying instead of doing. If he started out here, there's a good chance he's still somewhere on the farm. Mary and I will head out and start looking. You might want to call Kayla."

"I'll think about it. I'm sure we'll find him holed up somewhere and wishing he was home," Dylan said, trying to sound hopeful. She'd made her decision and left.

"It's your call. But she loves your little brother, and she

knows this property better than anyone."

"We'll probably have him back safe and sound before she could even get here from the city. We'll be okay without her." *Liar.* He'd never be okay without her.

An hour and half later, and there was still no sign of Derek or Patches. At least twenty people from town had already shown up to join in the search. Dylan was grateful for their help, but so far, they hadn't picked up any other clues, and they had to find him before nightfall.

It would be dangerous for him to be alone and unarmed with predators roaming the territory, including several coyotes that had been spotted not more than thirty miles south of here. Too close for comfort.

Lou's words rang in his ears for the hundredth time. *She knows the property better than anyone.* For someone who prided himself on not needing anyone, now wasn't the time for his stubborn pride to rear its ugly head. For Derek, he would call Kayla and beg if that's what it took, anything to find his brother.

Scrolling down his recent call list, he located her number, and pressed dial. He was surprised when she answered on the first ring.

"Kayla, it's me, Dylan. I need you. I, um, I mean, we need you. I know you don't owe me a thing, but I think Derek's run away with Patches, and we think he's on your farm somewhere."

"I already heard, and I'm sorry."

"You're sorry? That's it? I thought you cared about Derek. I promise to stay far, far away and never lay another hand on you if you'll help us. Please."

"I never said I wouldn't help. I was saying I'm sorry he's missing. Sorry I caused all this. I realize I shouldn't have interfered. You were right. Of course, I'll help look. In fact, if you get your stubborn self to my house in about ten minutes,

I'll meet you there and we can go look together."

"How? You father said you went back to Houston. And who are you calling stubborn? I'm not the one who left and who refuses to acknowledge what's still between us."

"First things first. Let's find Derek, and then we can talk. Deal?"

"Deal."

"My father called me right after Derek turned up missing, and I've been driving ever since. I love your little brother, and I'll do anything I can to help bring him home."

"Thanks. People are still showing up from town to help, but we can't have too many looking."

Dylan drove over to the Anderson ranch and waited. Kayla pulled in the driveway, a cloud of dust engulfing her SUV as it came to a sudden halt fewer than twenty feet from where he stood. She jumped out and made her way to his side.

"Get in the truck." Dylan didn't want to waste a single minute.

"I'll drive." Kayla's tone wasn't asking.

For once, he didn't mind her taking charge. Hopefully, she had better ideas than he did where to look for Derek. "Sounds good."

He'd tried not to need anyone, but the truth was, he needed Kayla. He needed everything about her. She understood him better than anyone.

"Thanks for coming back, Kayla. Any ideas?"

"A few. We'll pick some of the areas a little farther out since we don't know exactly what time he left. Dad said the others are starting in close and fanning out."

Kayla drove slowly through the fields and past the river. There was still no sign of Derek. As the minutes slipped by and dusk edged closer, the knot in his stomach clenched tighter and tighter.

She stopped the truck on top of a knoll and they got out

to scan the horizon for signs of movement.

They heard a bark seconds before they spotted the welcome sight of Patches bounding toward them. Their eyes met, hope reflected in hers, and it was a feeling he seconded wholeheartedly. He couldn't have loved Patches any more than he did in that moment.

"Where is he, boy? Can you show us?" Dylan hoped the dog would understand. Patches tugged at his arm in response, and Dylan was more than happy to let him lead.

"Wait, Dylan." Kayla stood looking in the direction Patches was trying to pull. She raised her hand to shade her eyes.

"I know where he's going," she said, her words laced with excitement.

"Quick. The old well shaft isn't far from here. Get in the truck."

Dylan scooped Patches up and held him tightly as he climbed into the front seat.

"Easy boy. We'll take you to him." He stroked the dog's head to calm him down.

Kayla looked over at him, a king-size smile on her face. "Glad to see you two getting along."

"Yeah, we sorta came to an understanding last night, but Derek didn't get the message. Let's hope he's okay." He said a little prayer for his brother, hoping he wasn't injured. Or worse.

"Step on it," he said, the image of Buster as he lay dying in his arms twisting his gut hard.

Kayla came to a skidding halt, twenty feet away from the old covered-up well. "We're here."

Dylan ran toward the opening and noticed a large piece of wood missing from the cover. "Derek," he called out desperately.

"Down here," his brother's voice echoed back up the

shaft. "My ankle hurts real bad, and I'm scared, and I'm sorry." Thank God, he was alive.

Dylan breathed a sigh of relief, but the jackhammer pounding in his chest continued.

"Hang on, Derek. I'm going to get some rope, and I'm coming down for you."

A silent look of understanding passed between him and Kayla. If it was only his ankle, they had a lot to be thankful for.

"Call the others and let them know, and I'll get the truck in position and hook up some ropes. You okay to drive and pull us out?"

"Is it safe?" she asked, her eyes narrowed in concern.

"If you drive forward slowly, I can walk us up the wall and out of the well. Understand?"

She nodded her head but still didn't look convinced.

He was ready by the time she hung up the phone. "I'm going down on the rope. I'll holler when you need to start driving forward."

Dylan dropped a kiss on her lips. "For good luck." He winked.

Dylan shimmied down the rope, relieved to see his brother in one piece. "I swear you took twenty years off my life. We'll talk about this later. Right now, we need to get you out of here and to the hospital to get that foot looked at."

A lopsided smile creased Derek's face and then quickly disappeared again.

"How's Patches?" Derek asked.

"He's fine. In fact, he led us to you. Special dog you have there. Reckon I ought to let you keep him." Dylan smiled.

"Really? You mean it this time?"

Ouch. "I mean it. And it's not because you ran away and worried me sick. I'd already decided to let you keep him, you know. I left you a note this morning."

"Oh. Okay." He shrugged.

Dylan had expected more than the nonchalant response he got. Maybe he was destined to never understand kids, or at least not his brother.

"You ready to get out of here?" Dylan asked when he finished tying the ropes for their ascent.

"Yup. I need to thank Patches."

"And Kayla," Dylan added.

"She's here? With you?" His brown eyes shot wide open.

"Yes. She came back from Houston the minute she heard you went missing. She's probably up there wondering what the holdup is." Dylan smiled, hoping his brother would give him a sign everything was going to be okay, but if his expression was anything to go by, there was still something troubling the kid.

"But why would she come?" he asked, his voice so low Dylan almost missed the words entirely.

"Because she cares about you."

Derek looked at him funny. "She cares about you, too."

"As a friend, yes." Stuck in a well with his injured brother wasn't the time or place for this conversation, especially not with Kayla waiting on them thirty feet above their heads.

"No. As more than a friend. I think she *like*, likes you. I've seen her watch you, and I heard her talking."

He took off his shirt to wrap Derek's ankle for the climb. "Oh. About what?" he couldn't help but ask.

"I heard her talking in the barn. Something about loving you. And something else about you. Something not very nice," Derek said, his voice trembling.

Dylan stopped immediately, shocked by his brother's words. He didn't know which part to focus on more, the loving or the something else. In the end, he chose the something else. Derek was fighting tears, and Dylan suspected it wasn't because of his foot.

His brother was obviously trying to understand something he'd heard, something bigger than he could understand, and he was failing miserably. The loving part was a conversation best had with Kayla, but it gave him renewed hope all wasn't lost.

"What else did she say? You can ask me anything. You and I don't have secrets," he said as he finished adjusting the ropes.

"Why haven't you ever told me you have a son?" Derek mumbled.

His question came out of nowhere, shocking Dylan speechless for a few seconds.

"I don't have a son. Where on earth would you get such a damn fool notion?"

"From Kayla." The two words slipped from Derek's mouth as if his source was beyond question.

"Kayla said I have a son?" he asked in disbelief, ready to strangle the woman waiting up above. Why would she say such a thing? "Surely you misunderstood her."

"I know what I heard," Derek mumbled in defense of his statement.

"I would know if I had a son. A man doesn't father a child and walk away. You know me well enough to know I take my responsibilities very seriously."

The first shadow of doubt crossed his brother's face.

"It's why I left, you know. I was upset thinking about you taking Patches from me, and then I heard what Kayla said, and I thought everything you've been preaching to me didn't apply to you, and that worst of all, if I had a nephew all these years, I wouldn't have been so lonely." It all came out in a rush, but Dylan understood every word.

"I'm sorry, Derek. I don't have a son."

"So why did you hurt her? She loved you, and I really like her. It'd be nice if she stuck around. Maybe you could work things out. Seems to me, a woman crying over you should mean something."

Smart boy for such a young age, and he managed to drive the nail right into the heart of the matter, not understanding the significance of his own words. Loved, as in past tense. Nothing with Kayla had been easy. More than ever, he was determined to make Kayla talk about the past and to find out why the hell she thought he had a son. It would explain some of her anger toward him, but not all.

"Ready to go?" Dylan asked.

"Yep. Moving around is making my foot hurt more." Poor kid was trying hard to be tough, but the grimace he tried to hide was probably closer to the truth.

"Next time, leave your shoe on. It helps hold down the swelling. Hold on tight around my neck and let me do all the work."

"Okay." Derek wrapped his arms around Dylan tighter than needed, but he welcomed the trust.

The discomfort was worth it if it meant Derek was coming home safe and sound. He yanked on the rope and called up to Kayla. "Pull us up!"

Chapter Fourteen

Inch by inch, Kayla edged the truck forward, stopping every foot or so to get out and check their progress. Ten minutes felt like hours, but finally, Dylan hollered for her to stop. Kayla latched on to Derek's arm to help pull while Dylan pushed, careful of his foot as they maneuvered him to safety.

She wrapped her arms around Derek, unchecked tears streaming down her face as she stood off to the side to watch Dylan pull himself up and out of the well.

"You gave us quite a scare, young man," she said, holding Derek tightly.

"Sorry. I, um, needed to get away to think." He looked away.

"You should have called me. I thought we were friends."

"Yes, ma'am." He was acting strange, but now wasn't the time to figure out what was wrong. Something had changed between them, and it left her with a cold loneliness she didn't like.

Dylan brushed off his clothes and hoisted his brother into his arms, leveling her with a hard look. "We need to get him to the hospital to have his foot checked. When he's settled in, you and I need to talk," Dylan said. The way he said it wasn't a question.

First Derek, now Dylan.

No smile, no hint of a smile, no nothing. She'd driven all the way here to help, and neither of the brothers seemed overly grateful. Even if giving Derek the dog had caused the problem in the first place, it was no cause for the silent treatment. But she would do exactly as Dylan demanded.

"Everything okay?" she asked, opening the door for Dylan to slide Derek onto the front seat carefully.

They both looked at her funny. "More or less," Dylan answered.

"Thanks for coming back for me," Derek said, his face tense with pain.

"Oh, honey, of course I'd come back for you. I just hope you don't do this again. I think you scared ten years off your brother's life." She grinned, trying to ease the tension in the air.

"He said twenty, so I reckon it just means a lot." Something had happened down in the well, and whatever it was, these two seemed a whole lot closer, but it also seemed to involve her. What, she couldn't imagine.

She pulled up to the front of the emergency room. Dylan carried Derek inside, and she went to park the truck. It had been a twenty-minute drive from the farm, but there had to be at least thirty people from town already here to see Derek. She knew every one of these folks, and yet she felt alone.

Kayla stepped off to the side as everyone assured themselves he was okay and offered their well-wishes while they waited for Derek to be called to one of the back rooms.

Derek was in his element with all the attention he was getting. Kayla scanned the excited crowd crooning over the boy and stopped when she recognized the face she didn't want to see.

Becky. The growing ache twisted deep in her gut when Becky touched Derek's face with tenderness. Whatever she said had the power to make the kid smile.

When Derek's name was called, Dylan carried his brother to meet with the doctor.

Kayla didn't belong here, and she shouldn't have promised Dylan she'd stay. The minute hand on the wall clock moved slowly. Ten minutes had passed, and it was more than she could take. The room started to close in around her. She needed fresh air. The doors slid open, and Kayla slipped outside and headed for the truck. Several of the town folk were already leaving, and she wanted nothing more than to be one of them.

"I'm glad you didn't leave," Dylan said from behind.

Lost in thought, she hadn't seen him coming. "How is he?" she asked.

"Sprained ankle. Nothing a few pain meds and the attention of several of the nurses can't handle." His half smile disappeared as quickly as it came.

"He's a lucky boy."

"Yeah, he is. I've only got a few minutes before I need to get back inside, and this probably isn't the time or place, but what we need to discuss can't wait another minute."

"Okay. Let's have it. I sensed something is wrong by the way you're both acting. Might as well get it out in the open."

"Well, for starters, why do you think I have a son? And why would you be talking about it with someone when Derek could hear you?"

Talk about being blindsided. She'd never told a soul about the baby. Kayla closed her eyes. *Dizzy.* Kayla thought she'd left the barn door open or a cat had been creeping around, but what if it had been Derek who'd run out and caused the door to slam?

And if so, how much had he heard?

She felt weak in the knees.

"Answer me, damn it." He towered over her, hands on hips. "For five years, you've treated me like I had the plague because I walked away after we made love. For five years, I've hoped you would come home, to me. Instead, I discover you think I have some secret son stashed away somewhere. Do you really think I'm that kind of man?" he asked, his voice cold.

"I don't think it. I know it." If he wanted to air the past right here and now in the parking lot of the hospital, so be it. Because then she was leaving. Back to Houston and away from everything Riverbend represented.

"What is it you think you know?" Dylan asked between clenched teeth.

Kayla saw the hospital doors slide open. Someone was coming their way, preventing her from answering. This wasn't intended to be a public argument.

Becky.

Great. Just what she needed.

"Hope I'm not interrupting, but there's quite a crowd gathering inside watching you and wondering what the two of you are heatedly discussing." Becky looked from her to Dylan. "Everything okay?"

"No. Everything isn't okay." Kayla was tired of everything being hidden away and yet never forgotten. She wanted to put it behind her, and maybe this was the way to finally move on.

"It hasn't been okay since you two hooked up behind my back down at the swimming hole. I was a fool to believe you could ever love me," she added, looking directly at Dylan, needing desperately to see his reaction.

But instead of the guilt she expected to see, his face was filled with confusion. Becky on the other hand, looked agitated. What the hell was going on? Had Becky never told

Dylan she'd seen them? It was unthinkable.

Kayla glared at Dylan. "Do the math, hot shot. Didn't it ever occur to you the timing of her son's arrival could make it yours?" There she'd said it. Let the cat out of the barn, so to speak.

Becky's face drained of color.

Dylan on the other hand appeared to relax.

"No, it never occurred to me, because I've never hooked up with Becky. Your words, not mine," Dylan said, a smile on his face.

Kayla glanced at Becky who still hadn't spoken.

"But I saw you both together, and Becky confessed," Kayla insisted.

Lines of tension re-creased his face, and his smile vanished. Dylan turned back to Becky, his stern gaze almost frightening. "How could you confess to something that didn't happen?"

Becky looked terrified and took a step back.

"I saw you with my own eyes," Kayla said.

"If you saw us, you should have stuck around for the finale, because there wasn't one. We kissed, and it was a mistake and we both knew it. For God's sake, tell her the truth, Becky."

"I can't," she stammered.

"You have to," Dylan thundered. "She needs to know the truth. Whatever it is you think you're doing needs to stop. Enough people have been hurt by the lie."

Tears streamed down Becky's cheeks. "I'm sorry, Kayla. He's telling the truth. We didn't sleep together. Byron isn't his son. When I confirmed your accusation, I honestly never expected you to think Byron was Dylan's."

"You admitted you were with Dylan down by the swimming hole."

Becky took a deep breath. "I was with Dylan, but not in

the way you seem to think. We kissed and stopped, just like he said. I felt guilty and came up to tell you what happened. I overheard you talking with your mom on the porch. I'm sorry I didn't tell you everything," she said, brushing away her tears. "We had dreams, and you were ready to take off and fly, and I had just found out my dreams had come to a crashing halt."

Dylan looked furious. The muscles in his arms flexed as he sought to maintain control.

"But why did you let me believe you got together with Dylan? I left and never came back because the thought of the two of you together nearly killed me."

"I let you think the worst because I overheard you tell your mom you would have stayed in Riverbend with Dylan. You would have given up all your dreams and been stuck in Riverbend forever, just like I was. I wanted you to have your dreams. We were so young."

"But it was my life."

"I know, and I'm sorry. But you're living your life. You're happy, right? It all turned out good, right?"

"No. Yes. I don't know."

Dylan's gaze feasted on her. "Repeat that last part," he asked.

"You heard me."

All these years and everything she'd believed about Dylan and Becky had been wrong. What did it all mean? So much had hinged on a lie. And then there was the baby. She still hadn't told him about the baby.

"If Dylan's not the father, who is?" she asked, finding it hard to switch gears.

"I can't say." Becky tensed. Something was very wrong. Kayla should have known. They'd been best friends. She should have trusted Becky, but instead, she'd failed her.

"But why? Someone should be helping you with the cost

of raising a child. Does the person even know?"

"He knows all right," Becky answered bitterly.

"Why are you protecting the guy?" Dylan asked.

"I'm not. I'm protecting my son. My family."

"What do you mean?" Kayla didn't understand.

"Has someone threatened you? Becky, you need to tell someone the truth. We can't help you if we don't know what you're fighting." Protective big-brother Dylan was emerging, and he would be a force to reckon with if fully unleashed.

"Please," Becky whispered, her eyes scanning the parking lot. "I can't tell you who, so don't keep asking. I made a mistake. I thought he loved me. Young, stupid, and naive. I love Byron and don't want trouble. Trust me, it's best if I never name the father."

"But it isn't right. Tell me so I can deal with the louse." Dylan wasn't backing down.

"Right is having my son with me. This guy could make my family's life hell, and I could lose Byron. Nothing is worth losing my son."

"I understand better than you realize." Kayla stepped in between the two. "Your secret is safe with me."

"This is ridiculous. Surely you two aren't agreeing to say nothing and let this guy get away with what he's doing."

"We do agree," Kayla said. "Two against one." Just like old times. She stepped closer to Becky and enveloped her in a long overdue hug. It had been wrong for Becky to control her future, but Kayla understood she'd done it out of love. *That* she could forgive.

"Damn it," Dylan said, the veins in forehead and neck popped out like a roadmap of rage.

All these years Becky had been dealing with so much on her own, made Kayla feel worse for leaving her best friend. Becky had done too good of a job driving her away and Kayla's pain blinded her to any other possibility. She'd make it up to Becky, somehow, some way, she'd make it up to her friend.

"I wish you'd told me. Maybe we could have fought this together like we did everything else. I wish you had trusted me with the truth."

"I do, too, but in the end, everything has worked out. Well, almost," she said looking back and forth between her and Dylan.

"Some things aren't meant to be, I guess. But you're lucky to have your son. He's a sweet boy."

"Thanks. Maybe you could drop by and spend some time with us, catch up," Becky asked hopefully. "But right now, I need to go back inside and get Byron before he wears old Mr. Thompson out with questions."

"Sure thing. I would love to stop by. And I'm sorry I ran off the other night at the wedding. Maybe someday I'll explain why." Thankfully, Becky didn't question the comment.

"Sounds good," she called over her shoulder, waving goodbye.

"You and I still need to talk," Dylan said. "I still can't believe you thought I would sleep with Becky and that I wouldn't acknowledge my own son."

"What would you have thought if you were in my shoes?"

"I would have cornered you and found out what the hell was going on," he growled.

"I was eighteen and inexperienced. And you were the first boy I'd ever kissed."

"I wish I'd been the first, the last, and the only," he said, claiming her mouth in a long overdue kiss.

And oh, sweet heavens, how the man could kiss. This was what Kayla had wanted from the moment he'd first kissed her all those years ago. Except she'd been here before with Dylan, and her life still wasn't in Riverbend anymore.

"You'll have to settle for first. But I have a question of

my own."

"Ask away, but understand this, last is still up for discussion," he said, holding her close.

"If it wasn't because of Becky, why did you walk away that day?"

"Same reason as Becky. To let you have your dreams. I knew you'd stay if I asked, and I didn't want you to give up everything when I had nothing. The ranch was failing, and I was tied to raising an eight-year-old boy. Not much to offer in exchange for your dreams. I'd always hoped you'd come back."

"But I'm not back to stay, Dylan. My life is still in the city."

"Life happens, and people change." It was the same thing her father had said. Five years ago, she would have given up everything for him and stayed, but it was different now. She was different.

"It's not that easy. Classes start in two weeks, and for the next year, I'll be slammed with schoolwork and clinic hours. And even when I'm done, there's no room for more than one small-animal vet in town." It was all true, but Doc had said some things that made her think twice about switching her specialty and coming home. But she wasn't saying a word yet because the thought of moving back to Riverbend terrified her.

And then there was her secret. The one Dylan would never forgive her for keeping.

"You can't leave yet," he said. "Derek will need help with everything for at least a week. I'm asking you to stay and take care of him. And the dog."

"There must be someone else who can help you?"

"I figure you owe me."

"How's that?" she asked, frowning.

"It's your fault he's laid up. He ran because he thought I

was taking away the dog you gave him without asking me. He ran because you left. And he ran because he thought I had a son I was hiding from him that he heard about from you."

You did have a son.

She had to tell him. "That's not fair."

"Life usually isn't." He grinned.

She did feel guilty, and when he put it that way, she had no choice but to stay. It was all her fault, and the thought of staying at the ranch for a week was more than enticing. Call her crazy, but she wanted to do it. It wouldn't leave her much time to get ready for school, but she could make it work.

One week of what it could have been like between them as a family. But she wouldn't survive if he kept kissing her.

"Only if you stop kissing me."

"I can't promise you that."

"Fine. One week. And then I'm going back to the city and to school."

"One week. Maybe a few kisses, and I'll change your mind about leaving."

Chapter Fifteen

The rooster crowed, alerting Kayla to the morning. A morning that came all too quickly considering the lack of sleep.

Dylan had been the perfect gentleman, and short of the disappointing peck on the cheek with a curt good night, he'd left her at her bedroom door and disappeared. She wasn't sure what she wanted, but her vivid imagination had a clue. A very good clue.

Her parents had watched her load her suitcase into the SUV and wave goodbye as she'd driven off. They weren't keen on the idea of her staying with Dylan, but it was more due to being old-fashioned than any real objection. They trusted him, and they loved Derek, but her mother had been quick to point out it was a very small town when you crossed moral boundaries.

But none of that mattered. Dylan was right. It was her fault, and it was the least she could do for him to make up for some of the mistakes she'd made. Not that anything would ever make up for all of them, but it was a start.

And how could she expect Dylan to forgive her when she hadn't forgiven herself? Her miscarriage had never been explained but she didn't need an explanation to understand the pain and heartache she would always bear.

Kayla wrapped a robe around her pajamas, ran a brush through her hair, and tried to wash away the bleary-eyed look she couldn't shake. She wondered how hard it would be to convince a thirteen-year-old to take a nap, because Kayla was certain she would need one before long. A note taped to the refrigerator confirmed Dylan had already left the house, giving her the time she needed to adjust. *Make yourself at home.* How likely was that?

Seven thirty. Either the hands on the clock moved super slowly, or she was super bored. Derek was still asleep. Patches had been out for a walk and was currently snuggled up in bed with Derek. She'd fixed breakfast for when he woke up, and the dishes were already cleaned and put away.

In the city, there was always entertainment to be found. Kayla settled on the sofa and picked up the *Cattleman Rancher* magazine and started to thumb through it. Page after page, she glanced at the advertisement and articles until one caught her interest.

Organic Beef, the Wave of the Future. One of her undergraduate classes had mentioned hormone-free, antibiotic-free, grass-fed cattle ranching as an up-and-coming trend. Kayla read and reread the in-depth article, an idea formulating in her head. One that would be a win-win situation for Dylan's ranch and her father's farm.

Her father had told her it was none of her business, and she'd let the matter drop, but it was impossible to walk away and not try to help while she was still in town. And if not for her father, she'd butt in for her mother.

Hours of research made the morning pass quickly as she worked through the details, putting paper and pen to the accounting and every other detail. Patches's bark echoed down the hall, and Kayla went to check on Derek.

"Hey, sleepyhead. Want some help getting downstairs? You must be hungry," she asked, discovering him awake.

"Sure. I'm hungry. What's for breakfast?"

"I made you some special pancakes we can heat up."

"Really? It's been a long time since I've had homemade pancakes." He pushed the covers back and started to get out of bed. "*Damn.* My foot hurts like hell," Derek cried out when his foot hit the floor.

"Hey, no call for bad language. I'm sure it hurts like a son of a gun, or even that it hurts like a two-ton bull stepped on your foot, but I can guarantee it doesn't hurt like H-E-double hockey sticks, because if it did, you wouldn't be here." She grinned to soften the lecture.

"Sorry, but what? You lost me," Derek asked in confusion.

"The only way to know what it feels like down there is to be down there, and since you're not, you have no idea. And I'm sure you don't want to find out. And guys shouldn't talk like that around a lady."

"Yes, ma'am. Sorry. But it does hurt like a two-ton bull stepped on it." He grinned.

He was a good kid. Nothing wrong with him a little love and guidance wouldn't fix, and since she was there for another week, it wouldn't hurt to lavish a little attention on him along with some of the guidance. Not that Dylan had done wrong by him, but a woman's attention was different. It was…motherly. Something she may never have a chance to experience again.

Getting down the stairs took some doing, but they managed it together, and once Derek was happily digging away at what she considered a huge pile of pancakes, she decided it was as good a time as any to head over to the barn.

"I'll be back in fifteen minutes after I check on the calves.

When I get back, you need to start on your schoolwork. I called the school and got all your homework assignments, so you don't fall behind."

"Gee, thanks." His lack of excitement wasn't surprising. No kid wanted to do homework, not any normal kid anyway.

"Anytime. That's what friends are for."

"To make my life he—heck?" He smirked.

"You guessed it." She laughed. Smart-aleck kid was just like his brother.

The first thing she noticed when she entered the barn was the quiet, followed quickly by the excessive heat. The fan in the corner of the barn sat silent, either switched off or not working. Her guess would be not working, because everyone knew it was important to keep the barn cool. She'd have to call Dylan, but first she wanted to check on the calves. Newborns were more sensitive to the extreme heat.

Wiping the sweat off her brow, she watched the calves suckle the dam. They seemed frustrated as they kept latching on and then letting go.

She called Dylan. "Hey, I'm in the barn and there's a problem with the fan and something's wrong with the calves. They won't take milk."

"I'll be there as soon as I can. Call Doc to see what he says about the calves."

"Gotcha. See you soon."

Ten minutes later, she hung up with Doc with a lot to think about. The heat had reduced the dam's milk production and increased the calves' need for precious nutrient-rich fluid. Double jeopardy. Until the fan was fixed, she needed to supplement the calves' milk intake with a bottle. That was the easy part.

Doc's other suggestion was more difficult. It was intriguing to say the least, but she wasn't sure how to deal with it. She was only here temporarily. At most, another week. But for that week he needed her help.

Kayla hadn't seen Doc in years, and the thought of him getting old was unsettling. The chance to help him would be amazing considering he was the reason she wanted to become a vet.

She still remembered the time Doc had saved Dizzy when she'd taken ill, and he'd been her hero ever since. It might have even been the moment in her life when she'd first become interested in working with animals, although she hadn't recognized it at the time.

All reasonable resistance had paled when she'd heard his arguments lined up, the last one designed to force her hand.

Doc was having heart trouble. No one knew, and he wasn't ready to let on yet.

She was here to take care of Derek and Patches, but how much would they need her? Helping Doc out would allow her to alleviate the boredom already setting in. It would be great experience, and who knew when it would come in handy.

She'd check with Dylan and Derek, and if they were okay with it, she'd do it.

"Hey there," Dylan called out as he entered the barn. "How's our patient?"

"Eating breakfast. But speaking of Derek, I need to get back to the house. I told him I'd be back in fifteen."

"He's got crutches, and he's not a baby. He'll be fine for a few more minutes. Tell me what you found out?"

"I need to supplement the cow's milk until you get the fan fixed. So get to it, because it's hot in here," she said with a laugh.

"I agree with you there. In fact, it's hotter in here than it is outside, but I suspect it has something to do with you." He grinned and swooped in to drop a kiss on her lips. "Good morning."

"Good morning to you, too, although morning's all but

gone." Kayla laughed. "What happened to the no-kissing rule?"

"I told you I wouldn't kiss you if you didn't want it. You looked like you wanted it and needed it. Double the reason, and double the pleasure."

He was right, but she wasn't about to let on and give him any more leverage. It was too easy for him. And what did he want? To finish what they started years ago, and then say goodbye again?

As interesting as Doc's offer was, her life was in the city and Dylan's was here on the ranch with his brother. And if she told him the truth about the baby, he'd probably kick her off the ranch faster than a herd of stampeding cattle.

"Why don't you go check on Derek and then come back and give me a hand?"

"You sure ask a lot from your free help."

"There's nothing about you that's free, trust me."

"I'm not sure how to take that comment."

"You'll figure it out if you stick around long enough."

"That's not going to happen. But I'll be back soon. I've got something I want to talk to you about anyway."

Thirty minutes later, she had Derek settled in on the couch with his homework.

"Why do you have to go back to the barn?" Derek whined.

"I need to talk to Dylan and help him fix the fan." It was partly the truth. The fan would probably already be fixed, but Kayla wanted to talk to Dylan about her idea.

Derek's demeanor changed instantly when she mentioned Dylan, and it wasn't hard to figure out why. It wouldn't be good to encourage the kid into thinking her and Dylan would get together and then for her to leave. She would have to be careful.

On her way to the barn, she tried to rehearse the best way

to pitch her idea to Dylan. It was a great idea for his ranch, even if the basis of the plan would benefit her family's farm.

Dylan shirtless was a sight she'd never grow tired of seeing. Hard muscles were carved into his back and down his arms, flexing as he worked on the fan, bent over and presenting her with an extremely nice view of his backside to boot. He hadn't heard her come in, and she chose to remain quiet for a few minutes, unwilling to give up the great view.

"Like what you see?" He stood and turned to face her.

"What are you talking about? I just got here."

"Liar," he said, closing the distance between them.

She took a step back.

"Are you and I are clear about Becky, my non-existent son, and the past?"

"Yup." She swallowed hard.

"Then let me make the next step between us perfectly clear." Dylan pulled her close to claim her mouth in a scorching kiss. This was no tentative, will-you-love-me-forever kiss. This was a heated kiss, full of desire. Strong enough to make her weak in the knees and want to beg for more.

She closed her eyes, relishing every second, drinking in every drop of heaven he rained down on her lips.

"Am I clear enough yet, or do you need more information?" he asked, his sexy cowboy grin warming her all the way to her toes.

She had to tell him.

"No. But there's something I need to tell you. About the past."

Something in her voice must have alerted Dylan, his smile fading in the space of a heartbeat.

"Is this the thing you've hinted at before, but wouldn't tell me?"

"Yes," she said, biting her lower lip.

A sneeze sounded from the corner of the room. Dylan

stepped back, his face tight with tension.

"Derek. Come on out." Hobbling along on his crutches, the kid at least had the good grace to look guilty. And he'd gotten an eyeful.

"Sneaking around and watching people is rude. Maybe if you're well enough to hobble on that foot out here, you're well enough to hobble around school, starting Monday."

"No, please. I'm sorry. I'd rather stay with Kayla."

"My mind's made up." Dylan could be firm when he needed to be when it came to Derek, but Kayla knew it was purely done from love.

"So unfair." He pouted.

"Unfair would be if I made you do your chores also."

Kayla had remained silent, stunned to discover she'd almost spilled her confession with Derek listening. She took a deep breath. "We can do fun stuff after school, I promise. Your brother's right. You're getting along on the foot pretty well, and it's easier to keep up with schoolwork at school."

Derek hobbled off, mumbling under his breath.

"Thanks for supporting me. It makes it easier."

"You've done a good job with him," she said. Now wasn't the time to talk about the past, but it was time to talk about the future of the ranch and the farm.

"But?" he asked, uncertainty in his voice.

"But you can't be everything all the time."

"I'd be lucky to be anything some of the time. The ranch takes up every free minute I have, and the rest is going through the motions of raising Derek. It's the best I can do."

"Which is what I want to discuss with you," she said. No backing down now.

"You lost me. I thought we were going to talk about the past."

"Right now, I want to talk about something else. I've been thinking about the problems on the ranch and farm and trying to figure out a way to make both work."

Dylan tensed. "I'm listening."

"The answer is for you to go organic. Sell off the herd and buy back fewer grass-fed organically raised heifers. You can run a herd almost a third smaller for the same profit margin. Organic beef sells for a lot higher price. Fewer cattle, less water. I read it in your *Cattleman* magazine. Your reservoirs could see you through drought years and the river allocation might keep my father in business if he agrees to an irrigation system."

"Won't work. There's a lot more involved than just selling off old cows and buying new ones. And it won't help anyone in the short term. Organic beef prices will eventually fall lower as more and more competition jumps in, and then we're right back where we started. For now, the problem is under control."

"You won't even consider it?" He was shutting her down without any real discussion. Just like her father.

"I already have. I'm not saying it's a bad idea, it's just not one I can seriously consider at this point. Moving the cows to the river was an easy, natural solution, and everyone benefited from the plan."

"I should have known you wouldn't listen. You and Dad are too much alike."

"I'll take that as a compliment."

"I'm not sure I meant it as one," she said, turning to leave.

"Stop. We're not done talking." He hadn't forgotten, and he wasn't letting her off the hook.

Chapter Sixteen

"Spill it, Kayla," Dylan said, closing the distance between them. "You can't leave until you tell me what you meant earlier."

"You'll want me gone after I tell you, but you need to understand, I was young."

"For God's sake, spit it out."

"I was pregnant when I left here. You did have a son. We had a son," she corrected.

His face drained of all color. "What the hell are you talking about?" He stood stock still, tension radiating from every pore of his body.

"I'm sorry," she cried, tears spilling from her eyes.

"Had? What did you do? And why didn't you tell me?" he thundered.

"I didn't do anything. At least not what you're suggesting. And I did try to tell you, but when I came home, I saw you and Becky together again and I found out she was pregnant. I left again without saying a word."

"You had no right to keep the pregnancy from me. What

happened?" He had every right to be angry.

She waited for him to order her to leave and never come back. "I miscarried."

Dylan walked away, his fists clenched. When he returned, his steely gaze never left her face. "I've heard it can happen early in first pregnancies."

"That's what they say. But I was early in the second trimester. It's why I know we had a son. They don't know what went wrong. I'm not even sure I can have more children." Kayla bit her lip, brushing away her tears with the back of her hand.

"I'm sorry I wasn't there for you. I would have moved heaven and earth to be with you, you know that, don't you?" he asked quietly. Too quietly.

"I didn't know anything except you walked away. No one knows. Not even my parents."

The tears in his eyes were like a window to his soul. He had every reason to hate her. Without a word, Dylan shook his head, turned and walked away.

Kayla returned to the house, threw a few of her things into a bag, and grabbed her purse. She would have preferred not to run into Derek on her way out the door, but no such luck.

"You need anything? I'm going to run over to the farm, and I'll be back later to check on you," she asked, trying to avoid eye contact.

"Is everything okay? You seem kinda weird." Kid was far too intuitive for his own good.

"I'm fine," she lied.

"Are you and Dylan fighting? Why do you guys always fight?"

She made the mistake of looking at him. The dejected look on his face twisted her own pain a little sharper.

"We just rub each other the wrong way. Always have, I

guess." She shrugged.

"You didn't look like you were rubbing each other the wrong way earlier," he said.

"Derek!" she scolded. "That's enough." She wasn't up to this level of conversation, especially not with a thirteen-year-old boy who couldn't possibly understand.

"I'll be back later to fix something for dinner unless Dylan has other plans," she said, attempting to force a smile and end the discussion. She had to get out of there before she broke down and cried in front of him.

Kayla walked the short distance to her parents', eager for the privacy of her own room.

Raised voices drifted down the hallway and caught her attention when she entered the house. Curiosity had her feet moving toward her dad's office when she recognized Dylan's deep timber. He had to have come straight here after their discussion, and it sounded like the two men were arguing, which didn't bode well.

If Dylan spilled the truth about the pregnancy to her parents, there would be hell to pay. She'd let them down enough, without them finding out her darkest secret.

She inched closer to eavesdrop.

The words "farm," "ranch," and "contract," bandied back and forth, and then she heard her own name. But nothing about the baby. She couldn't have left if she wanted to. Instead, she moved closer, pressing her ear to the crack.

"You have to tell her. I can't hold her off any longer. I don't like misleading her," Dylan said.

"No. If she finds out you own the farm, she'll be madder than a tornado and never forgive me. We agreed to the confidentiality clause, and the reasons for the clause haven't changed," her dad said.

Kayla sucked in a deep breath, covering her mouth to keep from being heard. Rage seethed deep within. It couldn't be true.

"But I can't keep lying to her. What happens to me when she finds out we've lied? Have you thought of that?" Dylan persisted.

"I'm sorry. You may own the farm, Dylan, but she's my daughter. I'm the one who stands to lose everything if it doesn't work out."

"I disagree." Dylan answered sharply. "There are some things more important than the land."

Dylan owns the farm.

Kayla heard footsteps coming toward the door. She scurried for cover, not wanting to be discovered and have them know what she'd heard. Not yet, anyway.

She couldn't believe it. The farm. The land. The river. Everything. *Gone.*

The snake next door must have done some mighty fancy footwork to get her father to agree, especially without telling her. What kind of deal had Dylan struck with her dad to steal what was rightly hers? All the pieces began to fall into place. Her father's resistance. Comments dropped here and there. Mr. Thompson's reluctance to help. No one wanting to do the work.

And to think she was living under his roof and had let him kiss her senseless.

Poor Derek. She couldn't give him what he needed, and he would be devastated when she went back to get the rest of her things, but there was no way in hell she was staying with his lousy snake of a brother another night.

Except staying here wasn't any better. Her home belonged to Dylan.

It hasn't been your home in five years. Had her dad been losing the farm and quit fighting to save it because she'd turned her back on it? Had selling been the only solution, and if so, why was he still living there? It didn't look like they were on the verge of moving out.

It hurt that her dad hadn't bothered to discuss it with her. *You made it clear you were never coming back.*

It was her own fault. And she hadn't planned on coming back, at least not until recently.

Being home, she'd come to appreciate a peacefulness about the place she hadn't remembered. It was her home, and she missed it. *But enough to come home for good?* She'd never know the answer because now, there was no home to come back to.

Chapter Seventeen

A knock on her bedroom door the next morning intruded into Kayla's trip down memory lane as she lay there thinking of the years she'd spent in this house. Her entire childhood. All she wanted was to be left alone, but apparently that wasn't going to happen.

"I know you're in there, Kayla. Answer the door." She knew from experience her mom wouldn't go away until she answered.

Resigned to the intrusion, she opened the door. "What's up?"

"Dylan's here and wants to talk to you."

"No. There's nothing for us to say." Her mother's jaw dropped open in shock. Kayla couldn't blame her for the confusion. She didn't know the truth.

"Kayla Lynn, you march down those stairs and be nice. He's done a lot for our family, and whatever he's got to say, I think you should hear him out."

She closed her eyes and took a deep breath, exhaling at a snail's pace. "Fine." Only it wasn't fine. It would never be fine again. There was no way she would ever consider moving home if Dylan owned the property. *Stole the property is more like it.*

Kayla followed her mother down the stairs as if she were being led to the guillotine.

Her dad and Dylan were on the porch talking in voices low enough she couldn't hear what was being discussed.

Hands on her hips, she faced Dylan. "I've been duly summoned. What is it you want?"

They might force her to talk to him, but they couldn't force her to be civil. The promise she'd made to her father had been before she knew the truth.

"I'm sorry. Can we take a walk and pick up the conversation where we left off last night?"

"What conversation? The one with me, or the one with my father?"

Dylan's jaw clenched. She didn't miss the quick glance he sent her dad.

"You heard us discussing the property?"

"Your property. Tell it like it is. You're a low-down, conniving jerk who somehow managed to convince my father to sell the family farm. I heard every word. Make no mistake, I plan to find a loophole or something to prove you cheated my father. He would have never sold the property willingly."

With each word, she'd stepped closer and closer until only inches separated them and she could use her finger to poke him in the chest to emphasize her point.

Dylan grabbed her hands and pulled her hard against his body to hold her still. "You're wrong. You were wrong about me before, and you're wrong about me now. I love you. Everything I've done has been because I love you. But I'm done. I can't do this anymore."

"You love the property," she said, but the words rang hollow.

Was it possible he was telling the truth? She wanted to believe him, but how could she? She'd been wrong before. Did she owe it to him to listen? *No. Not this time.*

Dylan looked at her father. "Show her the damn contract."

"I can't. We agreed. It could change the outcome," Lou said.

"It will change the outcome if you don't," Dylan said quietly.

Her father shrugged. "I suppose."

She was missing something in the exchange between the two men.

"And don't worry about my brother, Kayla. He's my responsibility, and I've got him covered. Thanks for your help." He turned to walk away.

Not again. A sense of déjà vu hit her, her heartbeat an echo of the emptiness she'd felt once before.

But this time he wasn't walking away, not without getting a piece of her mind. "That's it?" Kayla called after him.

He paused and turned back to face her.

"What do you want from me?" he asked.

The resignation in his voice caught her off guard, but it wasn't enough to stop the words from pouring out. "You tell me you love me, and then walk away. Again? How is this any different than the last time?"

"Last time, I set you free to find your dreams, hoping they would lead you back to me. This time, I'm setting you free because you've found your dreams, and they don't include me."

"Says who?" she asked.

"Says you and your dream of being a small-animal vet in the city. Says you and your accusations about my motives in buying your father's land. Coming home for Sophia's wedding hasn't changed a thing." Dylan tipped his hat and turned to leave.

His words gave her pause, but it didn't change the fact he owned her family home. Something her father would never have allowed without good reason. She looked at each of her parents, who hadn't said a word. Her mother's eyes glistened with unshed tears. Her father's expression was unreadable, but the stiff set of his shoulders said volumes. Dylan kept walking toward the barn where his horse stood tethered.

"Everything he's done has been for you. Trust him, Kayla. And if you don't trust him, trust me," her father said.

"What's in the contract that's so important?" Her father was still defending Dylan, giving her cause to wonder why he wasn't upset about the sale. Her dad suddenly smiled, as if coming to a decision.

"Nothing important that can't be fixed. It all depends on you."

"What?"

"You used to love him. Your mother and I knew it back then. The question is, do you still love him?"

She closed her eyes, the question sending her into a tailspin. Her heart had always known the answer, and no matter how hard she'd tried to lock away her feelings, the key had always been in Dylan's possession. It's why she'd stayed away.

But everything had changed now. He hadn't slept with Becky, and they didn't have a son together. He'd walked away to give her a life, not destroy it. And she'd told him about the baby, and he still claimed to love her. No recriminations. No anger. No blame.

It all came down to trust, because otherwise, the choice was easy. She liked the city, and she liked the country, but she loved the cowboy walking out of her life.

"I do." The words squeaked out. She always did. Always would.

Her father let out a huge sigh of relief, his smile genuine.

Dylan had mounted his horse and ridden away without a backward glance.

"Then I reckon I ought to tell you about the Kayla clause."

Nothing could have prepared her for the explanation, but by the time her dad was finished, Kayla understood everything. If she came home of her own free will and decided to stay, the farm was hers for the bargain price Dylan paid her father. He stood to lose everything he'd put into saving the ranch and the farm if she moved home and reclaimed the homestead. And there was only one reason he would have done it.

Love.

And she'd let him walk away. He'd proven his love in a way far greater than she could ever imagine, and in return she'd stomped on his heart because she hadn't trusted him. Both men had been equally determined to let her make her own way in the world, determined to put her happiness first, all the while hoping her journey would lead her back to Riverbend and her home.

"Thanks for telling me, Dad."

"What are you going to do about Dylan?" he asked.

It wouldn't be easy, but she had to find a way to prove her love *and* her trust.

"I'm not going to run away from a second chance with the first and only man I've ever loved. I just need a few days to work out the details for a lifetime."

• • •

Hard work the past two days was the only thing that gave Dylan relief from the heartache ripping him in two. Heartache over Kayla and heartache over the baby. Her news had been like a bomb going off, destroying everything he believed about the choices he'd made five years ago. And nothing could turn back the hands of time to undo the damage he'd done.

Dylan had laid his heart on the line, not quite the way he'd planned, but it had all been pointless. It had been a gamble, and he'd lost. She'd believed the worst about him years ago, and obviously, nothing had changed. But then again, she had every right to hate him.

Years of hope had been wiped out in the space of one conversation.

He hadn't heard a thing from anyone at the Anderson place. It was a good thing Derek had gone back to school, because he couldn't take twenty-four-seven of the kid asking about Kayla and why she'd left.

Patches barked from the front room, alerting Dylan he had a visitor. He wasn't expecting anyone, but it wouldn't surprise him if Derek had gotten into trouble at school based on his attitude at home the past couple of days.

He swung the door open after the first knock.

"Hey, Lou. What's up? Is everything okay?" It wasn't often Lou showed up on his doorstep in the middle of the day.

"Kayla asked me to deliver this note."

"What's it for?" he asked, relieved she was okay.

"Not my place to open it or ask. But I can tell you this, save yourself the hassle and just open the letter and do what it says. If there's one thing I know for certain, son, you pay attention when the women folk talk. It's a whole lot easier."

Lou raised his hand in farewell and was gone.

Dylan unfolded the note.

Meet me at the tree house at three p.m.

A little over an hour. Even without Lou's expert advice, Dylan would be there. Wild horses wouldn't keep him away.

At three o'clock sharp, Dylan arrived at the tree house. Underneath the big oak, Kayla stood waiting, as beautiful as ever. His heart beat in a staccato rhythm, thumping harder in his chest with each step that closed the distance between them.

"Hey. Thanks for coming." A gentle smile teased at the corners of her mouth.

"What can I do for you?" he asked. It wouldn't take much for him to break down and kiss her even though it was the last thing she would have wanted from him. She'd made her point quite clear. But it didn't stop a man from wanting what he couldn't have.

"I wanted to tell you I'm moving home." The words he'd waited forever to hear.

He should have known. What he hadn't counted on was the reality of what it would mean, having to face her day after day but not being with her.

"I guess that means your dad told you about the Kayla clause in the contract. Welcome back. I'm sure your mom and dad are very happy."

"I haven't told them yet. I wanted to work out some issues first."

"What about your schooling and the partnership?" Mundane conversation between two people when, at least for him, things were anything but mundane.

"I'm going to apprentice with Doc for my clinic hours, and the university is letting me take the last two classes online. I've already called the other partners in the clinic to rescind my acceptance of their offer." She brushed her windblown hair off her face.

"I see. Sounds like you have it all worked out." Everything he could have hoped for, except the part where he didn't get the girl.

A rumble sounded from close by. Dylan caught sight of storms clouds moving toward them at a rapid pace. He stepped out from under the tree for a better view. "Looks like rain. You better be getting in the house, and I better be getting back on home. And thanks for letting me know."

Kayla moved to stand next to him instead of heading for the house.

"There's one other thing. I saw an attorney this morning." It explained the envelope she was holding.

"You aren't wasting any time reclaiming what's yours." It all came down to the water rights. If she owned the land, they were hers to do with as she pleased.

He eyed the storm clouds bearing down upon them. They needed the rain desperately, and this storm looked like it was going to deliver.

She handed him the envelope with a pen. "I need you to sign this."

"Is this about the herd? I'll have them moved within the week." Dylan pulled the paper out of the envelope and glanced at the attorney's logo across the top and the subject line. *Re: Purchase Contract between Dylan Hunter and Lou Anderson. Section V. 1. Kayla Clause.*

He trusted old man Smith since he was the attorney who drew up the original contract, and he trusted Kayla even more. She was the one who had a problem with trust.

Dylan scrawled his signature across the line marked with an X and handed the document back to her.

"I'm not sure moving the herd is in our best interests at this time."

He couldn't have heard her right. "What do you mean? What will you do with the farm?"

"I don't own a farm." She looked up at him, her blue eyes piercing him with their intensity. "I'm not here to be a farmer. Or a rancher. I'm a veterinarian."

"I don't understand."

"Do you ever read papers before you sign them?" Her hint of a smile had turned into a full-blown grin.

Always. Except where she was concerned. He glanced down at the copy of the document he held in his hand and started to read. *A cancellation notice.* They'd cancelled the Kayla clause. The farm was still his.

This wasn't what he'd expected. What had she done? The contingency plan he and Lou had ironed out to save the farm for Kayla in the event she chose to return was history. He owned it all outright.

"Why would you do this?" he asked.

"The same reason you would agree to such a ridiculous clause when you bought the farm in the first place."

He knew why he'd done it. Dylan was afraid to believe she meant the same thing.

"Why did you?" Her soft voice touched a chord, calling for the truth.

"All I ever wanted was you." He'd sworn not to go this road again, but he wouldn't lie, even if she stomped on his heart again.

"And if that didn't work out?"

"I don't know. Switch to raising organic cattle and back to having water hauled in, I reckon." He shrugged.

"You said you love me. Did you mean it?" she asked.

"Yes. But—"

"Good, because I'd like to apply for the position of rancher's wife."

Her shocking words wrapped around his heart and squeezed.

"I wasn't aware I was hiring. Besides, it's not the life you wanted. Not to mention the little matter of trust. Without trust, a relationship is empty."

"I do trust you. The document you're holding proves it. I'm giving you everything because I believe in you, and I believe in us."

She was putting everything on the line. For him.

"I'm sorry about what I said. I didn't mean any of it. I was angry no one bothered to tell me about the contract or that you owned the land. It was easier to make you the bad guy, but it doesn't make it right. I don't hate it here. I thought I did. But being back home has shown me things I didn't understand, because I never came home long enough to see what was right in front of my face."

Dylan fought against the wave of hope threatening to break free. "Like what?"

"Like, home is where the heart is. And mine is here with you. It's always been here. Not in the city. Not at the farm, but with you. You and Derek. I love you."

She stepped in close, wrapped her arms around his neck, and pulled his head down, searing him with a kiss much like the ones he dreamt about for years. One hot enough to start a fire if it weren't for the rain beginning to fall.

Rain. They both stopped and looked up with awe.

Light at first, until the bottom dropped out. Then it began to pelt their upturned faces, drowning them with the glorious and welcome drops from heaven. The leaves on the oak tree rustled in the wind, the big, heavy limbs groaning in protest.

Kayla stepped back and swirled around, her hands held high. She laughed as the torrential downpour fell, soaking them.

"I've waited forever to hear you say those words." He kissed her forehead, her cheeks, and then went back to her lips. She'd been completely honest with him, and it was time to return the favor. After they got out of the rain.

"Let's go up." He pointed to the tree house. Back to where it all started between the two of them. Back to when he first knew he loved her.

Kayla grinned and made her way up the ladder. Dylan followed her protectively, admiring the view all the way to the top.

Once inside, he took her in his arms for another soul-satisfying kiss before he stepped back. She deserved the whole truth.

"When I walked away five years ago, it was partly to let you chase your dreams, but there was another reason. I didn't want you to become like my mother. I watched how the ranch destroyed her, but I've learned a few things along the way, too. My dad wasn't one to trust others to help him get a job done, always working from sunup to sundown. He was never here for my mother. He was as much to blame as she was for the way things worked out. I'm sorry I let their choices interfere with our future. With what we had between us. Most of all because it kept me from being there for you when you needed me the most. I don't deserve your forgiveness or your love, but if you give me both, I'll spend a lifetime proving to you it's the right decision."

"I already know it's the right decision."

His heart felt so full he thought it would burst. "I promise you I won't be like my father. I'm going to promote Leroy to foreman, so I can have more time with you and Derek. Like a real family. Are you sure you ready for this?"

"Yes, it doesn't get any better, because we'll be together. My cowboys are all I need. The city was a poor substitute for what I needed most. You."

Dylan dropped to one knee. "Well then, Kayla Lynn Anderson, I'd like to offer you the job of rancher's wife. Your duties will be to love me for all the days of your life."

"And what do I get as payment?"

"My love, for all the days of *my* life."

"Sounds reasonable."

Dylan stood, pulling her into his embrace. Kayla was back in his arms, this time forever.

Epilogue

Four years later

"It won't be long, and you'll be off to Dallas and breaking hearts at the university. Emily's going to miss Uncle Dewek," Kayla said, copying Emily's mispronunciation.

"Can't say I'm going to miss the stinker. Follows me around everywhere." Derek grinned. "Not to mention the diaper duty coming up when the new baby gets here. I've done more than enough of mucking stalls and cleaning this little girl's dirty diapers to last me a while."

Kayla rubbed her belly at the mention of the baby due to make his arrival in three months. Her surprise pregnancy with Emily had been fraught with worry even with the doctor's reassurances everything should be fine. It wasn't until she held Emily in her arms that she'd stopped worrying. And through it all, Dylan had been by her side, full of love and understanding.

"You know you loved every minute of it. Her adoration, not the dirty diapers." She laughed.

Derek had grown into a remarkable young man, and she was going to miss him being around all the time. It was his turn to leave home and make his way in the world. She only hoped he wouldn't stay away as long as she had when she'd been his age.

"Maybe, but don't tell anyone. It would ruin my image." Derek put Emily up on his shoulders and galloped around the room playing horsey, her squeals of laughter filling the room.

Patches lay curled up in the corner, enjoying the spot of sunshine beaming through the window.

"Sounds like someone's having fun," Dylan said.

Kayla's heart did a somersault when she spotted her handsome husband standing in the doorway.

"Daddy! You home." Emily held out her arms. Dylan crossed the room to pluck her off Derek's shoulders.

"Yes, honey. Daddy's home in time to read his little princess a bedtime story." Dylan moved to Kayla's side and wrapped his arm around her, dropping a kiss on her mouth. "Hi, sweetheart. How's my girls and the little man?" He caressed her swollen belly. His touch still had the power to make her heart race.

"Doing great, thanks to your brother. I'm not sure I want to let him leave." Her young brother-in-law had been a great kid, and was an even more amazing young adult. Emily couldn't have a better uncle.

"Thanks for your help the past few days, Derek. I wouldn't have felt comfortable running the cattle drive if I didn't have you here."

A silent look of understanding passed between the two men. Derek had turned out just fine, and she knew Dylan was proud of his brother. Everything was exactly as it should be, and she knew without a doubt Derek would be home to stay one day. Once Riverbend was in your heart, there was no staying away.

About the Author

Elsie Davis discovered the world of romance at the age of twelve when she began avidly reading Barbara Cartland, and she's been hooked ever since. An award-winning author, she writes contemporary romance and romantic suspense. Elsie writes from her heart, hoping to share a little love in a big world.

Three daughters, four grandchildren, and her own hero husband, keep her extremely busy when she's not glued to the keyboard. She loves Caribbean cruises and the great outdoors.

Indoors, she enjoys a toasty fire, a glass of red wine, and of course, a great romance with a guaranteed Happily-Ever-After.

Find your Bliss with these great releases...

The Cowboy's Homecoming Surprise
a *Fly Creek* novel by Jennifer Hoopes

Single mom Peyton Brooks's first Friday night out—with adults—in forever isn't exactly going the way she'd expected. She can line dance at the local dive bar with the best of 'em, but she can't shake the feeling she's completely out of her depth. Then the first man she ever loved walks in the door, bringing chaos, especially since the handsome cowboy's the father of her daughter. This definitely calls for whiskey...

The Bookworm and the Beast
a novel by Charlee James

Shy, bookish Izzy is happy to accept a job as a temporary assistant, until the grumpy author claims he didn't actually hire her. He might be as handsome as a storybook prince, but his prickly personality and resistance to all things Christmas are sure to make for a chilly holiday season. Derek soon realizes Izzy could be the perfect solution to his interfering family this Christmas...if she'll agree to pretend to be his live-in girlfriend.

His Outback Nanny
a *Prickle Creek* novel by Annie Seaton

Jemima Smythe is over the world of fashion and she is determined to show her hometown she's ready to put down roots. Three boisterous kids in need of a nanny offer her an opportunity. But their smoking-hot dad, Ned, offers her another—become his wife, as a matter of convenience only. Not a bad arrangement, if only they can stick to the rules of their strictly-business marriage—no kissing and absolutely no falling in love allowed.

Opposing the Cowboy
a *Hometown Heroes* novel by Margo Bond Collins

Yoga teacher LeeAnn Walker has no desire to see her grandmother's ranch violated by a greedy oil company. But unless she finds the paperwork confirming she owns the mineral rights, that's *exactly* what could happen. The worst part? The guy spearheading the whole mess is none other than the hot and sexy stranger LeeAnn just kissed to make her ex jealous. Jonah Hamilton thought his day was looking up until he found out the gorgeous blonde who kissed the hell out of him is the same stubborn woman he came to town for.

25863529R00121

Made in the USA
Columbia, SC
05 September 2018